MONA & MASON

THE PARANORMAL CHRONICLES

VOLUME 1

AMANDA SIEGRIST

Short Stories

Paint By Murder

Follow Me, Sweet Darling

Sleighville Novel

Dashing Through the Fear

Here Comes Chaos

The Last Noel

Standalone Novel

The Danger with Love

———

Conquering Fear Novel

CO-WRITTEN WITH JANE BLYTHE

Drowning in You

Out of the Darkness

Closing In

THE DOLL HOUSE

A MONA & MASON MYSTERY - #1

A Special Note

This story was written during Halloween 2018 using writing prompts from the lovelies in my reader group, Love & Happy Endings. Every week, they gave me a prompt and I would write a scene to go with it. Within the span of about two months, Mona and Mason were born. Each chapter is titled with what prompt was used that week, except for the very last chapter, Time to fight more evil. That chapter is a never before seen chapter.

This is just the beginning of many more stories to come with Mona and Mason and the mysteries they will solve. I sincerely hope you enjoy this short story! I want to give a special thank you to Jane, Melissa, Isadora, and Deborah for providing me with such amazing prompts! I couldn't write flash fiction without you lovelies! So thank you from the bottom of my heart.

Happy reading!
♥ Much love, Amanda Siegrist

WHY DO YOU LOOK WEIRD?

"They say Old Man Bennett was bludgeoned to death with a sledgehammer while he was sleeping."

"No way. It was with an ax."

"Dude, you're both idiots. It was a baseball bat."

"I heard it was a golf club."

The three boys standing in her way jumped, screaming. She held back her laughter, amazingly enough, when all three boys stared at her with wide eyes.

Leaning forward, she lowered her voice to a whisper. "It was a putter. He was hit so many times, no one could be sure it was him. His face had been obliterated."

"Who are you, lady?" the oldest boy said. At least, she assumed so by the way he straightened up as tall as he could with an air of confidence the other two boys lacked.

Propping a hand to her hip, she smirked. The evil smirk she liked to use with her old neighborhood boy who liked to throw pebbles at her car. "I'm the new owner of this house. So, I would say I know how the story goes."

The two younger boys' eyes grew even rounder.

The oldest boy jerked, yet held his stance. "You actually

bought this house? You know it's haunted, right? Old Man Bennett roams around, groaning and moaning."

"How would you know? Have you ever been inside?"

The boy shrugged. "Everyone knows that."

Mona glanced at the house. The lawn looked like it had been neglected for a long time. It stood at least two feet tall. She'd have to hire a lawn service because she wouldn't be breaking her back to mow that crap. The steps looked worn, cracked paint, but sturdy. Hopefully, anyway. This was her first time visiting it.

She almost started laughing hysterically.

She bought the damn house without even looking at it.

As she perused the entire outside of the house, it looked like the whole thing needed a new coat of paint. A bright white or maybe sunny yellow. Because, as it stood now, with black and gray peeling paint, it looked just as dreary and haunted as the boys claimed it was.

Who painted a house black and gray? So odd.

But so was her impulse to buy a house she had never seen before.

This was what she got for trusting her real estate agent. She was always a sucker for helping people out, especially someone she considered a good friend. When her friend said she couldn't sell this house, even if she sold her soul, she told her she'd buy it.

Never again. How could she be so stupid?

The windows were dirty, filled with grime and...was that soot? Had there been a fire inside?

Next time she'd have to turn a blind eye to a poor soul and look at a house before she purchased it.

Yet she had wanted to escape. Flee far away from all her problems.

It looked as if she'd fled straight into new problems.

"Why do you look weird?"

Turning her attention back to the older boy, she arched a brow. "Why are you a rude little boy? Perhaps I'll tell Old Man Bennett to pay you a visit..." She leaned closer. "While you're sleeping."

All three boys jumped back as the older boy said with a shaky voice, "You're crazy, lady."

"No, I'm your worst nightmare." She cackled, pretty decently if she did say so herself, and then whispered, "Boo."

The boys didn't stick around for more. They turned and fled down the sidewalk.

"I am crazy. Already making enemies of the neighborhood boys. Why do kids hate me?" She glanced around, noting the street and sidewalk was empty. No one would be answering her question.

With her house surrounded by two fields, yet the other side of the street layered with a few houses, she knew she wouldn't have many visitors. Except if they wanted to catch a glimpse of Old Man Bennett. At least two of the other homes looked like they were for sale. Nobody wanted to live in the neighborhood.

She laughed out loud. "Haunted. Yeah, right. Just what I need." Grabbing her suitcase from the backseat of her car, she started up the walkway. "You and me, Old Man, better get along. I get cranky when I'm hungry, I don't like to share the remote control, and when I'm cleaning, I like my music loud. I'm just throwing that out there."

She paused at the bottom of the porch stairs. From a distance, they looked sturdy. Closeup, she had concerns her feet might fall through.

"And weird? Who asks that kind of question?"

Glancing at her outfit, she rolled her eyes. So maybe she

was dressed a bit weird. She had on an orange tank top with black straps and a floral skirt with patches sewn around here and there. Her mother made it for her. She feigned happiness when her mother gave her the present but secretly hated it. Her mother never did care what others thought. Growing up had been difficult with a carefree mother who did and said weird things.

Oh, no. She just acted like her mother.

Since her mother recently passed away, she didn't have the heart to throw the outfit out or anything else her mother had ever given her. When she found the clothes hidden in the bottom of her drawer as she packed up her stuff, she put it on. She instantly felt closer to her mom.

So maybe she looked weird, a little mismatched.

She apparently bought a haunted house.

She scared the local kids.

She got fired from her job. Which really wasn't her fault. How was she supposed to know her new supervisor had been married? Lost and confused after her mom died, she fell into his arms without thinking about it. Well, his wife sure cleared up the confusion. And the president of the company further solved that dilemma by letting her go. Because, of course, her new supervisor was married to his niece.

Bad luck.

That was her life.

Wherever she went, bad luck followed.

"It's just a house. A silly, stupid house that my friend couldn't sell because it looks like shit on the outside. That's all."

Pep talk firmly done, she let out a big breath and climbed the porch steps. Surprisingly, they felt very sturdy, although they looked rotted to the bone.

Unlocking the door with the key her friend gave her, she pushed open the door and stepped inside.

"Did I walk into the right house? Because this doesn't look right. I should stop talking to myself, too. That makes me even stranger."

Barely stepping away from the front door, she glanced around the foyer. A large foyer that appeared clean and dust-free. A large, winding staircase was in front of her with a big, gleaming chandelier hanging above. To her right looked like the living room furnished with a white couch and two small, decorative chairs. They looked extremely uncomfortable. To her left, a small room, maybe a parlor. Wasn't that what it was called? She had no idea, but she liked the idea of calling it a parlor, receiving her guests there first with a sweet treat.

And she was getting distracted with fanciful ideas. Nobody would probably visit her.

She also noticed a hallway that she assumed would lead her to the kitchen.

Everything looked clean and pristine. Did her friend hire a cleaning crew? Based on the decrepit look outside, she expected to see the same inside.

"I can work with this. I like this."

Meow.

Screaming and jumping, she twirled to her right to see a black cat.

Hand over her heart, she laughed. "I don't do cats. You're going to have to leave, big fella."

Meow. Hiss.

Taking a step back, she stopped when she realized she was retreating. "No way. I'm the boss here. Not you. You get out."

The front door slammed.

Jumping again, this time toward the staircase, she looked at the front door, then at the cat. Strangely enough, the cat looked at the door and then at her.

"The wind did it."

The cat stared at her, its bright-green eyes glowing as if it knew something she didn't. Something she should know.

Yeah, like Old Man Bennett haunted the place.

"Look here, Old Man. It's my house now. Not yours. You and the black cat better pack your shit and go. I'm crazy, if you haven't noticed."

There. That would show everyone—cat, ghost, hell, even the tiny spiders she imagined lingered in the dark corners—who was the boss around here. Because she was done letting people run all over her. Even a cat and a ghost. No way would they be running her out of here.

A door slammed upstairs.

Meooooow.

Between the cat and the door slamming, she needed a drink.

"It's only the wind."

Nodding to herself that it couldn't be anything but the wind, she set her suitcase down and headed for the front door to grab more of her belongings. Like the box full of her liquor supply tucked away in the trunk.

When she twisted the knob, it wouldn't budge.

Meow.

"Is this why the house never sold? Because once you step inside, you never leave."

Meow.

"Oh, shut up. Dumb cat."

A cold hand touched her shoulder.

Shrieking, she turned around and faced—nothing.

Nobody stood there.

Instead of letting the fear take over, she let the anger consume her. Because if she was going to be stuck in a haunted house with a bludgeoned dead man and an annoying black cat, she could've at least brought in the box with the liquor and snacks.

She was hungry, damn it. And nothing good ever happened when she was hungry.

FROM OUT OF NOWHERE

He leaned against the banister and grinned. Well, he feigned leaning against the banister. If he actually leaned against it, he'd fall right through. Not that it hurt to go through things because it didn't. In fact, he couldn't feel anything. Not a damn thing. Which was why he never went through walls, doors, or leaned against something because it unnerved him that he couldn't feel it.

Sometimes, being a ghost sucked.

Well, no, that wasn't true.

It sucked all the time.

"Come on, you stupid door." The woman with the prettiest black hair he had ever seen turned his way, then back at the door.

He straightened.

Why did she look his way? Did she sense him? Did she know she wasn't alone? He tried to touch her, then backed away before his hand went through her shoulder. Not to mention, he had scared her, and that was the last thing he wanted to do.

She grabbed the doorknob once more and pulled.

Glancing down at Scatter, the black cat that roamed the house, the only other living creature that could see him, he shrugged. "Should we tell her she has to wiggle the handle, then lift it to open the door?"

Meow.

She whirled around. "Don't start with me, cat. Shoo! Go away."

He looked right at her as if she would be able to hear and see him. "His name's Scatter. He only responds to that."

Shaking off a shiver, she turned toward the door and kicked it. "I refuse to be defeated by a dumb house." Turning his way, she shouted, "Open the door, Old Man! Don't make me show you my crazy side."

He grinned and chuckled, sharing a look with Scatter. "She's cute angry, isn't she? And what old man is she talking about? I'm not that old."

And he wasn't. Not even close. He was thirty-five years old. That wasn't considered old, or was it? Times could've changed. What did he know?

Sure, he'd been dead for the past fifty years, but he died when he was thirty-five. That didn't make him old because he still looked thirty-five. He hadn't aged.

He didn't do anything but wander around the house, talking to a cat like a crazy person, and contemplate why he was stuck in the dumb house.

She was right.

This house *was* dumb.

He cocked a brow at Scatter. "Am I old? Is your silence saying I'm old?"

Meow.

From out of nowhere, the woman stalked his way, stopping a foot away. He jumped, something he hadn't done in years.

"Stop meowing. It's like you're mocking me. I've had enough mockery in my life lately. I'm not going to let a stupid cat do it to me, too."

The sad look in her eyes made his heart ache. Why such sadness? Who put it there?

His hand lifted and reached toward her, stopping short of caressing her cheek. The sudden need to touch her overwhelmed him. The feeling was odd, unfamiliar.

He hadn't felt anything in forever. Not in touch. Definitely not in feelings. He knew nothing about this woman other than she didn't scare too easily, and he wanted to comfort her in any way he could.

Before he could fulfill his urge to touch her, not that he'd be able to feel her anyway, she turned around and walked back to the door.

"You shut without notice and now you won't open. What's the deal? I need my food. I'm seriously hungry." She twisted slightly and arched a brow at Scatter. "You got any food, buster?"

He laughed again, loving her strange reaction to everything.

When the door slammed, he expected high-pitched screams and manic behavior, which usually occurred when it happened to other people. And it happened a lot, especially every time a new realtor tried to sell the house.

It never sold.

Until her.

It wasn't him, of course, who slammed the door. He wasn't a cruel ghost that roamed the house. Not to mention, his hand would just fly through the door if he tried to touch it and slam it.

He honestly couldn't explain why the door shut on its own. In all his time here, he never saw any other ghost.

But that didn't mean he didn't feel a presence.

Because there *was* something else here.

He just didn't know who...or what it was.

The skin around his eyes crinkled with amusement when she snapped her fingers at Scatter, who sat next to him watching her just as intently.

"You are of no use to me, cat. Go away if you're not going to help open the door or bring me some food." She looked past him, up the stairs. "Where are you, Old Man? Bring me some food if you're not going to let me escape."

He crossed his arms. "I'm not old, and I'm not holding you here against your will. Simply wiggle, then lift. It'll work, I promise. Happens all the time."

She huffed, then twisted back toward the door and grabbed the knob, jerking hard on it. "Let me out."

He looked down at Scatter, his lips curved with a crafty smile. "I almost hope she doesn't figure it out. We haven't had this much excitement in a while. I like her." His grin intensified. "I really like her."

Meow.

The silly grin on his face wouldn't disappear as he watched her ignore Scatter's latest sound and struggle with the doorknob. She had a nice shape. Tall and willowy, as if she were a dancer. Long black hair that looked as fine as silk. And her eyes. Bright-blue eyes, like the sky on a beautiful sunny day. She had a strange outfit on, but it didn't detract from her beauty. He had never seen such a beautiful woman in his life. And back in the day, when he was alive, he had his fair share of women. Even a dancer one time, who could do the most amazing things in bed.

Could this woman? Was she a dancer as well?

What was he even thinking? He was dead. She couldn't see him. Pondering such things was a useless endeavor.

His smile died in its place as the realization hit him. He'd only be able to look, never touch. Never talk to her and find out her name.

Such a simple thing. A name. He'd never be able to ask her what hers was.

He wouldn't be able to reach out his hand and say, "Hi, I'm Mason. Nice to meet you."

She needed to leave. Just like the rest always did. She couldn't stay. He was already living a life of torture by roaming this house with no answer to why.

With three large steps, he was by her side. Before he could think about it, or even remember he wouldn't be able to help, no matter how hard he tried, he reached for the doorknob where her hands were twisting with rage.

His hand touched hers. It didn't glide through but actually touched.

She froze.

He froze.

Then she screamed.

BELLS WERE RINGING

JUMPING IN HER SPOT, something she never did because not much scared her, she whirled around. Nothing stood before her.

But something had touched her hand.

Someone.

"Who's there?"

Determined to show she wasn't frightened, although she had acted that way, she put her hands on her hips and curled her lips into a sneer. Well, as close to one as she could manage. Her nerves were still shaking from that touch.

A very cold touch.

But a touch, nonetheless.

Maybe this house was truly haunted by Old Man Bennett.

When nothing stepped out of a wall, or a low moan bellowed her way, or even another cool touch to her body, she lowered her hands.

A tiny laugh escaped.

"Mona, you're acting ridiculous. This place isn't haunt-ed." She started to laugh a little harder.

Nothing touched her. Nothing could've touched her. Because ghosts didn't exist.

Meow.

Twitching slightly, yet thankful she didn't completely jump in her spot, she glanced down at the dumb cat. "Don't start with me, buster."

Meow.

Narrowing her eyes into tiny little slits, hoping to scare the cat away, she didn't move a muscle. Her expression turned wary as the cat walked closer and brushed against her leg as if saying hi.

She shifted away.

"Don't do that. I don't like cats. I told you that."

The cat didn't listen as it stepped closer and brushed against her leg again.

"Knock it off."

It became a game of sorts. She would step back, and the cat would keep coming, trying to brush against her leg as if demanding she accept him as a friend.

But she didn't want a cat for a friend.

She didn't like cats. Never had. Not even as a little girl when the neighborhood cat, that everyone loved to feed but not bring into their home, was friendly with everyone. Everyone but her. It even scratched her one time when she tried to pet it.

Dogs loved to bark at her, too.

Animals just hated her.

This dumb cat was probably trying to gain her trust so he could get closer to bite and scratch her.

Not going to happen.

As she kept stepping back and the cat kept advancing, she finally found nowhere to go when she hit a wall.

Shivering, she made a mental note to check out how well this place was insulated because standing against this wall felt like an iceberg.

Then a strange sensation swept through her body. A tingling feeling she had never felt in her life.

It didn't feel like a wall anymore. It felt like a pair of hands grasping her hips and a solid body leaning into her.

Slowly turning her head, she gasped as she stared into a pair of bright-amber eyes. She ran right into the most handsome man ever—not a wall. She couldn't even turn around fully to get a better look, she was stunned in place.

"Can you see me?"

Her mind blanked as the man stared back at her with awe.

Wait a minute.

How did he get into her home?

What did he want?

Was he going to hurt her?

And what the hell did he mean could she see him? She wasn't blind. Of course, she could see him. All the delicious parts, starting with his golden-hazel eyes, to his soft-looking lips, to his gorgeous dark-brown hair that looked made for her hands to comb through. Oh, and he had a beard. She always did have a small fantasy to date a man with a beard.

The man looked away, down at the cat, and grinned. "I don't think she can see me, Scatter. But she must sense me. You rascal. You did this on purpose."

Cocking a brow, she scoffed. "What the hell are you talking about? How did you get in my house?"

He jerked his gaze back at her, his mouth wide open

with surprise. "You can..." His hands, which were resting lightly on her hips, tightened. "You can really see me?"

"Buddy, I can feel you, too." She glanced down at his hands gripping her sides, then back at him. "You should get your paws off me before I call the cops."

His brows furrowed, then he nodded. "My apologies."

He stepped to the side and let go of her.

He disappeared right before her eyes.

Twirling around, her gaze darted back and forth.

Nothing stood before her but a wall.

A very solid, very sturdy wall.

"You're losing your mind, Mona."

Walking backward toward the front door, hoping against hope it'd open for her this time so she could escape this mental house, a low cry slipped from her lips as she tripped over the stupid cat.

She had no time to stop herself. She fell to the floor, landing hard, her head banging against the wooden floor.

Bells were ringing in the distance, her brain rattled from the hard hit. Her vision blurred. She blinked a few times to regain her composure.

She wanted to move, but it hurt. Her head, her back, her butt. Everything just hurt.

"That man, a figment of my imagination, was right. This is all your fault, you dumb cat."

Meow.

Groaning at the cat's annoying response, she didn't try to see where the dumb animal was.

"All I wanted was to move away for a new start. Not deal with more crap."

She closed her eyes.

A cold hand touched her cheek.

She instinctively knew it was the man again. The same

one that disappeared right before her eyes. She slowly opened her eyes and met his warm, hazel gaze. So much concern sparkled in her direction.

She had to be losing her mind. Seeing things.

"You're not real."

He frowned and let go of her cheek. He disappeared in a flash.

Odd. Why was it every time he let go of her she couldn't see him? She missed his touch. True, it was a cold touch that always sent a chill straight through her spine, but it was also a gentle touch. It made her feel...something. She couldn't quite grasp the right word.

"Hello? Strange man?"

She sat up, taking her time. She finished what should've been an easy task, sighing heavily. Her body screamed in protest, her head pounded, a slight ringing still echoed in her ear.

"Are you there? Touch me again."

Nothing.

No cold touch.

No beautiful hazel eyes gazing at her.

Just silence.

Meow.

And the dumb cat.

She looked at the cat and glared, then gradually moved her lips into a frown. Lifting her hand, she held it out toward the cat. "Scatter? Is that your name?"

Meow.

The cat came closer, rubbing its soft, furry body against her hand.

A sweet smile touched her lips. "Where'd the man go, Scatter?"

The cat answered by jumping into her lap and sitting

down.

Shocked, and touched for the first time an animal wasn't trying to maim her, she wrapped her arms around him.

"I've lost my mind. I think I hit my head so hard I imagined a handsome man right before me." Her smile grew as a gentle purr sounded in her ear. "But that can't be right. It's just you and me."

She let out a sigh.

"I'm officially a cat lady." A strangled laugh let loose. "Scratch that. I'm a crazy cat lady."

WOULD SHE DATE A GHOST IF SHE COULD?

HE MADE sure to stay back a good distance from the woman cuddling with Scatter on the floor.

Rubbing his eyes to make sure he was seeing things correctly, he almost huffed in response that Scatter was in her lap. That darn cat never went near humans, other than him, of course. In fact, Scatter loved to hiss and claw at people when they stepped inside the house.

So why was he acting all nice and lovey-dovey with this woman?

With...Mona.

He was pretty sure she called herself that in one of her brief mumblings. It was difficult to remember everything she said because he was still reeling from the fact she could see him. Really see him—feel him.

He felt her. She had been warm to the touch with the softest skin imaginable. And in the last fifty years, that was all he'd been able to do when he saw a beautiful woman venture inside the crazy house—imagine what her skin would feel like.

It rarely happened. Not many people came inside so he

could appreciate the view of a gorgeous woman, or just being around other people.

But not with Mona.

Why could she only see him when he touched her? He had no answer for that, and it bothered him. He wanted to touch her again, just to make sure his theory was correct. That he needed to be touching her in some small way for her to be able to see and feel him.

Oh, how he missed talking to another soul. Making eye contact and seeing the recognition in a person's eyes that he wasn't a figment of their imagination but real. An honest-to-goodness real man.

But was he a real man?

Could a ghost be considered real?

When he touched her, he was as real as when he had been alive. That was enough for him.

He wanted to touch her again. Talk to her. Have her look straight into his eyes and...smile, maybe.

Would she smile at him?

Would she let him touch her so they could have a conversation?

Would she date a ghost if she could?

Wait. That last question was silly. He didn't even know why he thought such a ridiculous thing.

"Get off her lap, Scatter. You're making a fool of yourself."

Meow.

He almost stomped his foot like a petulant child when Scatter responded, yet didn't even look at him when he meowed. Well, if that wasn't a brush-off, and by a cat, no less.

Who was the real fool here?

Him.

Jealous of a cat.

How much more foolish could he be?

All he had to do was kneel beside her and touch her arm, and then she could be in his arms instead of holding Scatter as if she never wanted to let go.

Turning away from them, he blew out a deep breath. "You are not jealous of a cat. You're not." Glancing up the stairs, he nodded. "I'm out of here, Scatter. I'm done with her. You do whatever the hell you want."

He took a step forward, then stopped when a low meow echoed his way.

"If I touch her again, I'll just frighten her. She doesn't even believe I'm real. You heard what she said the last time I touched her."

You're not real.

She was right. He wasn't. It didn't matter he felt real when he touched her; he wasn't. He was a ghost. And ghosts couldn't be real, solid things.

Meow.

"I can't, Scatter. Come on already. Let's leave her alone."

He took another step toward the stairs.

Meow. Hiss.

"Oh, you darn cat. What's your problem?" Mona said with a small cry.

He turned around, surprised to see Mona on her feet and Scatter standing between them.

Hiss.

"Don't get that tone with me, mister." He wagged a finger at Scatter.

"Scatter?" Mona said tentatively. "Do you see something? Is it something bad?"

He looked away from Scatter to see a slight fear in Mona's eyes.

No. Anything but that. Because that would mean he scared her. He put the fear in her eyes.

"Do you see what you're doing, Scatter? You're scaring her. Knock it off."

Meoooooow.

Mona took a few steps his way. She stood so close, if he reached out, he'd be able to touch her. "Hello? Old Man Bennett? Was that you I saw? Are you here with me?"

He rolled his eyes. "Definitely not this old man you keep talking about. It's Mason. My name is Mason." Looking down at Scatter, he shook his head. "And if I touch you, my sweet Mona, I could tell you that. I'd also scare you even more."

Scatter suddenly jumped on the back of Mona's legs, making her lose her balance. He had no choice but to put his arms out to stop her from falling.

Warmth instantly invaded his body as her hands curled around his biceps. He stood as still as a statue as they stared into each other's eyes, his hands resting lightly on her waist.

"I'm not sure whether I hate that cat or love it yet."

He cracked a smile. She always reacted in the least way he expected.

"You feel real. Yet when you..." Her hands tightened on his arms. "Don't let go. You always disappear when you let go."

He had no idea what to say. She wasn't screaming, running in the opposite direction.

Her brows furrowed low. "Do I have bad breath? Am I scaring you? I know you can talk."

"You're beautiful."

Sweet laughter fell from her lips. He couldn't believe he blurted out such a thing. Yet he wanted to hear her delightful laughter again.

"Well, that must mean my breath doesn't stink."

Definitely not. He wanted to lean closer and kiss her. Find out how sweet she tasted. How would she react if he did? Would he be able to touch his lips to hers? He had to believe he could, since he was touching her right now.

"This isn't awkward." She laughed again. "At least tell me your name."

He smiled. "It's Mason. And I hope I'm not frightening you."

She tilted her head. "I have to admit, this is a bit odd, but it takes a lot to scare me."

"You see a ghost and it's only a bit odd. I like you, Mona."

Her hands loosened, but she didn't let go. "How do you know my name?"

His hands, which had settled on her waist as if they belonged there, tightened. "You were talking to yourself earlier. I just assumed..."

A low laugh escaped. "I forgot. Favorite pastime of mine, talking to myself."

"I like it." He glanced down at her hands, then met her gaze once again. "If I let go..."

"I know. We could...hold hands and talk. This is...a little weird how we're standing."

He started to let one hand go from her waist when a door slammed upstairs. Mona jumped and hugged him, her tiny arms wrapping tightly around his body.

"There's more than one of you? Are they as nice as you?" she whispered, clearly telling him she was more afraid than she had admitted.

Slowly glancing up the stairs, his arms tightened around her. "I honestly don't know, my sweet Mona. Last time I checked, I was the only ghost living here."

ON ANY OTHER DAY

IT'S as if she were surrounded by snow, an avalanche thrown right on top of her. As much as she wanted to control her shivering, she couldn't. The cold was seeping into her bones, making it impossible. And yet, she didn't want to step out of Mason's arms.

For the first time in a very, very long time, she felt secure. Content almost.

And he was a silly ghost. It made no sense.

If there was another ghost floating around the house— not that Mason floated—it looked like he was a flesh-and-blood person when he was touching her. But if there was another ghost in the house, one even Mason didn't know about, she was more than happy to stay right where she was.

In his cold, chilly arms.

"I should step—"

"No." Her arms tightened around his waist. She pressed her head firmly against his chest, trying to make it as difficult as possible for him to step away.

She should be running from him. Screaming in hysterics. Acting like a normal human being would when faced with a ghost.

Instead, all she wanted to do was hold him and never let go. So odd.

Why did she feel this way?

His hand brushed up her back lightly. A strong shiver rushed down her spine at the contact.

"Mona...I'm making you...you're freezing."

Well, she had a winter coat tucked in one of the boxes in the trunk of her car. She could always put that on. Then she wouldn't shiver as much and she wouldn't have to leave his arms.

Except she couldn't escape.

Wait.

If she managed to open the door, it'd be crazy if she came back inside. No matter how safe and wonderful it felt to be in Mason's arms, she couldn't stay here. She couldn't keep this house full of mystery and spooky things.

A nice ghost was one thing, but a mean one?

The door that slammed didn't sound friendly at all.

There was a reason her friend could never sell this house, and now she knew why.

She might be a proud homeowner for the first time in her life, but she wouldn't be living here. She couldn't.

Acting brave in the moment was different from being brave full time. And Mona was far from courageous.

Just look at her life. She always ran. It was easier to run from her problems rather than face them head-on. Any sane person would agree. They would.

Or not.

Was she truly sane right now?

She was hugging a ghost and didn't want to let go, even with his kind suggestion she should because he was turning her into an icicle. Her fingers clutched tightly to his waist were starting to go numb.

"I should go check out that noise," Mason whispered.

Another tremble coated her body at his frosty breath that touched her neck. A dose of fear washed over her as she thought about him leaving her side.

"It was probably nothing. It was the wind."

A low chuckle almost soothed her rattled nerves. "It wasn't the wind, Mona. And I don't like that I'm making you shiver. We should just hold hands or something."

Closing her eyes as she tightened her grip, not that she could get it much stronger, she clung to the one thing in his voice he probably hadn't meant to reveal.

Hesitation.

He didn't want to let her go.

Just like she didn't want him to let go.

"How did you die, Mason?"

His body stiffened.

Regret settled in her stomach like a nasty virus about to make her explode. Why did she blurt such a question? So rude. *Way to go, Mona.*

"I didn't mean to say that. Forget I said anything."

A soft sigh released as Mason brushed another light hand up, then down her back. "I honestly don't know. I can't remember. I only remember walking into this house for...some reason that I can't remember now. The next thing I knew, I was dead. An apparition. A ghost. A thing nobody can see." He paused, his hands tightening on her back. "But you. I've never been able to touch a single thing without passing through it, except for you."

A mystery. Didn't the unknown bug him? It would bug the hell out of her. It bugged her right now. A deep, sudden need to solve how he died came over her.

Which meant she had to leave and do some research.

"How long have you been here?"

"Fifty years. Why?"

Lifting her head, she met his gaze. "Don't you want to know why you died? Don't you want to remember?"

"Not if...I guess I do."

Eyeing him quizzically, she tried to decipher what he meant to say. "Not if, what?"

He looked away. "Nothing."

"I'm like a mosquito. I'm gonna keep trying to suck you dry until you swat me dead."

His head whipped back in her direction with a tiny grin upon his handsome face. "What?"

She brushed a hand over his smooth, yet scruffy beard just because she couldn't resist. It was sexy as hell, enhancing his already gorgeous features.

But she couldn't let herself get distracted.

"I'm going to annoy you until you either tell me what you said or you—"

"Kill you?" A brow rose as a silly smile emerged. "That's the most preposterous thing I've ever heard."

"Well, I wouldn't go as drastic as killing, but you could shove me away. That sounds just as brutal."

His smile died. "You're freezing to death with me holding you. That is killing you, in a way."

Dropping her hand, Mona looked away, unable to handle the sadness in his eyes. She disliked seeing that melancholy expression. "How did this conversation start? Let's move on."

"You started talking about mosquitoes. But I agree. Let's move on. I should go check upstairs."

Her heart started to pound. Could he feel it? Did he feel

anything? Was she cold to the touch for him? Why was he so eager to let go?

Maybe she misheard the hesitation in his voice. Maybe this was her acting like her typical self. Reading a situation completely wrong. Story of her life.

She met his gaze once more. "I should...go get my winter jacket. That would help."

His brows lowered into a frown as more sorrow coated his eyes. Then, like a light switch, a smile graced his face. "Splendid idea. You grab your jacket while I check upstairs. I'll meet you back here."

"Just one problem."

"What?"

"The house won't let me leave."

He chuckled. "It's a finicky handle. That's all. Wiggle, then lift. It'll open."

One arm slipped away from her back as his other hand grabbed one of hers. He slowly walked her to the door and nodded at the doorknob. "Go on. Try it."

Before she could talk herself out of it, she grabbed the knob and did as he said. Wiggled, then lifted. The door swung open.

His smile looked strained for a brief moment before it shined brilliantly. "I shouldn't be long. And you? Maybe grab a few boxes while you're out there. One with food, perhaps."

She giggled, remembering her earlier tantrum complaining she was hungry. On any other day, she would've never forgotten how hungry she was. But embraced in Mason's arms, everything else, all her problems, had disappeared. Only he existed. "Yeah, of course."

"My sweet Mona, I..." His words died as he let go of her hand.

Nothing stood next to her. Not a solid, real man. Just empty space. She didn't even see the dumb cat, Scatter.

Time to go.

Stepping outside, she shut the door, then headed for her car.

Not to unpack.

But to leave.

She was never coming back.

She'd miss Mason, but she would never step foot inside that house again.

SHE WAS TIRED OF LETTING FEAR RULE HER

Not if...

He was certifiably crazy that he almost admitted to her he didn't want to know why he died if it meant he'd finally cross over to the other side and leave.

That meant he'd leave her.

He just found her.

Or met her. Whatever you wanted to call it.

What did one call these things these days?

He felt as if he'd been hit in the head with a two-by-four so hard, it knocked all this desire and love for her in one fell swoop. Especially when they touched.

Oh, he couldn't even describe how wonderful her touch felt. Warm and soft. So warm. It made him feel like a real man.

Until she shivered and it let him know his touch made her cold.

She made him warm.

He made her cold.

So many mysteries. Ones he would eventually figure out.

Because he might not remember why or how he died, but he remembered what he did for a living.

He was a detective. A very good one, if he did say so himself.

Which was why he would figure everything out, especially who slammed the door. Because if it meant he could keep Mona, he'd solve every mystery he could.

Stopping at the top of the stairs, he glanced down the darkened hallway, then looked at Scatter, who stood by his feet waiting for him to make the first move.

"What do you think? Which room did it come from?"

Meow.

"I agree. It sounded farther down the hallway. Maybe the last room on the left."

Five bedrooms waited before him to be searched. Three on the right, two on the left. The bedroom closest to the stairs was empty. The other two bedrooms on the same side of the hallway had a small bed, one dresser, and a toy chest. One was decorated all in blue, the other all in pink. He assumed kids had occupied them at one time. The other two rooms on the opposite side were also furnished with beds, but much bigger, as well as a larger dresser. The very last room, the one he thought the noise originated from, besides the bed and dresser, had a rocking chair and twelve display cases of dolls. Each doll stood in its own case, pretty as a picture in a beautiful dress and their hair combed and curled to perfection.

Twelve cases.

Twelve dolls.

Each wearing a different colored dress.

The room creeped him out. He never ventured inside.

"By all means, Scatter, lead the way."

Meeooow.

Huffing out a breath, he nodded, his lips in a grim line. "You're right. Mona could be back at any moment, and I don't want to be late meeting her downstairs. I want good news for her. Like, it was the wind."

If cats could arch their brow in a mocking way, he figured that's how Scatter was looking at him right now. Because what he said was ridiculous. It wasn't the wind. It was...that thing. That presence he knew was around but never revealed itself. He minded his business, and the presence, or whatever it was, minded theirs.

He took a step forward and then stopped, looking at Scatter. "You do think she's coming back, right? Would you after meeting a ghost?"

His heart skipped a beat. Well, it felt like it anyway, even though his heart hadn't beaten in years. He was dead. How could his heart beat?

Slowly looking back at the staircase, agony tore through him. Gutted him straight to the core, making him wish he could cross over. Disappear into a whole new world.

Because Mona wasn't coming back inside. Why would she?

Straightening his spine, he surged ahead with quick steps to the one room he dreaded entering but knew he had to. So she wasn't coming back. That was fine. He still needed to find out who—what—was living in the house with him. He needed to make sure he and Scatter would survive...

Survive what?

A horrible sensation pulsated through his veins as the nasty thought hit him. Something bad was going to happen.

His hand hovered around the door handle. Glancing down the hallway, a tender smile touched his lips. "Don't come back inside, Mona. For your own safety."

Blowing out a breath, he dropped his hand, realizing he

wouldn't be able to open the door, and stepped through it instead.

He heard Scatter pawing and meowing on the other side of the door, but he did nothing but stare in horror at the scene before him.

———

"DON'T DO IT. It's crazy. Don't do it."

Mona paused in her pacing right outside the front door and stared as if, if she stared hard enough, she'd be able to find the answer she was looking for.

What would happen if she walked back inside?

It sounded like a simple question. But it was the furthest thing from the truth.

Would Mason reappear? Would his touch eventually give her hypothermia and she'd die? It wasn't that strange to contemplate, especially since his touch earlier turned her lips blue. She was shocked when she saw herself in the rearview mirror.

Her hands had held the steering wheel, the key in the ignition, her foot on the brake pedal.

And she sat frozen.

Just staring at herself in the mirror.

Then, after staring for what felt like hours, she turned off the car, grabbed her winter jacket from the trunk and some snacks from the backseat, and walked back to the house.

She owed Mason a good-bye. Not a slap in the face by ignoring him. He had been kind. So very nice and sweet.

And a dumb ghost.

Why did the first man who seemed like a great guy have to be dead? Life just wasn't fair.

Resuming her pacing, her eyes darting frequently to her jacket and food resting near the door, she tried to find the courage to walk back inside.

She was tired of letting fear rule her.

She had to stop running from every difficult thing that occurred in her life. Where did it get her? Nowhere but to new problems.

Right now, her problem was a handsome, sweet ghost that made her shiver like an icicle. And she couldn't leave him wondering why she left without a good-bye.

She couldn't live here, but she could have the decency to explain why she was leaving.

Or she could stop acting like a coward and ask Mason more questions, find out why he died. Maybe help him...see the light.

"Why hasn't he crossed over? Maybe he's here for a reason. What reason?" Closing her eyes, she almost screamed out her frustration. "Just go back inside, Mona."

Nodding several times, confirming to herself she could do this, she snatched her jacket from the porch, then grabbed the bag of chips and gummy worms she would inhale the minute she opened it.

"You can do this."

She placed her hand on the doorknob and swung the door open before she could chicken out. Stepping inside the house, she shivered. Not from a cold spot either, as if Mason were near.

More like she sensed something... malevolent.

"Mason?" Looking around, she couldn't see him, or even Scatter. "Are you here? Did you check out the noise?"

The door slammed behind her.

Screaming, her jacket and snacks fell from her hands as she jumped away from the door.

A tiny strangled laugh escaped. "Don't be a ninny, Mona. The door did that before. It probably has a loose hinge or something. It's nothing to be scared about."

Another shiver raced up her spine when a whisper of a hand brushed across her cheek. Jumping back again, her eyes round with fright, she glanced up the staircase and screamed, "Mason!"

Because she knew the hand that touched her hadn't been Mason.

She also instinctively knew Mason would save her from...whatever stood before her.

Swiveling her gaze away from the stairs, she looked straight ahead. "What do you want? Because my boyfriend's here and he's gonna kick your ass."

Whatever evil thing stood before her—and she knew it wasn't a nice spirit—they didn't need to know that Mason wasn't her boyfriend, or even real. But, as another ghost, he could kick this spirit's ass. Mason appeared strong and healthy. Well, for a ghost. What did she know?

Nothing. She was letting the fear control her. Crazy things always came out of her mouth when she got scared.

Releasing a tiny breath, she tried to relax her features and smiled. "You don't scare me. Whoever you are."

Tiny goose bumps flushed her skin, letting her know whatever stood near her was coming closer.

Another scream tore from her lips when a blur of black jumped right by her head.

Scatter, the annoying cat, but now her hero, hissed and scratched through the air in front of her.

She didn't stick around to figure out what he was fighting. She turned around and fled up the stairs.

THE DOLLS ARE REALLY DEAD PEOPLE THE MALEVOLENT SPIRIT ACQUIRED

MASON BRACED HIMSELF, hoping he'd still have the magic touch to hold Mona as she came barreling his way down the dark hallway. She screamed as she collided with him. Her hand started to swing his way, as if defending herself.

"Mona! It's me, Mason. It's okay. What happened?" Mason wrapped his arms around her, his heart splintering at the tiny murmurs of terror that fell from her lips.

Burying her head in his chest, she squeezed him. Only her heavy breathing echoed around the hallway.

Her warmth, the heat that radiated all around him, soothed some of his weary nerves after the scene he witnessed in the room. But by her silence and the shivers coating her body, she was far from calming down.

"What happened?" he whispered the question he didn't want an answer to as he glanced down the hallway.

He sensed nothing coming their way, nor did he see anything. That didn't mean something wasn't making its way toward them.

Where in the world did Scatter disappear? He normally waited for him when he walked through a door because

Mason couldn't open it for him to follow. Not that he walked through many. He and Scatter usually stuck together.

Leaning away, he kissed her forehead. "Mona, talk to me. What happened?"

He waited with a strained breath for her to look up. When he held her, touched her, it felt like he was truly breathing. His heart thudded. His nerves tingled with anxiety. His entire body felt warm and alive.

When she finally met his gaze, it all took a severe nosedive, his heart slamming to the floor with excruciating pain. The fear etched in her beautiful gaze broke him where he stood. He'd do everything in his power to keep her safe from...whatever frightened her. But would he be able to? Unless he was holding her, he couldn't control anything. Hell, he wasn't sure if he could control anything even touching her. Would he be able to open a door while holding her hand?

"Mona? It's odd you're not talking. I need you to say something."

"You have to pretend to be my boyfriend." Her eyes rounded with shock.

He couldn't hold in his surprise at her odd words. Then a tiny grin appeared as more warmth filled him up.

"I could probably handle that task. But may I ask why?"

She shrugged as a small smile started to form on her gorgeous face. "I might've told the..." She shrugged again. "Whatever is downstairs you're my boyfriend and you'd kick its ass. You should go do that. Like, right now."

Another tremble rushed throughout her body, sending a tingling sensation down his spine. And not in a good way. A terrifying way.

"What did you see?"

A sad frown touched her lips. "Nothing." She squeezed

the back of his shirt, her fingernails grazing his skin. "I didn't see anything, but I felt it. Then Scatter came out of nowhere and started clawing at the air, hissing. I just ran."

When another shudder rippled throughout her body, he pulled her closer, kissing the top of her head. Then he tensed, as Scatter came running toward them, the hair standing straight up on his back.

"Come on."

Mason had no idea what to do, but he felt exposed and unprotected standing in the middle of the darkened hallway. Grabbing her hand, he pulled her toward the last door on the left, and without thinking about it, grabbed the handle.

Shock touched him, but he didn't stop to enjoy the amazement that he actually opened a door. For the first time in fifty years, his hand touched an object and moved it.

Pulling Mona inside the room, waving his hand at Scatter to come inside as well, he shut the door quietly.

"Umm...Mason...what is..."

Turning around to what Mona had to be looking at, he wanted to slap himself in the head. He should've picked a different room to hide in, but this had been the closest one.

Standing all in a row in front of the bed were the twelve dolls that should've been locked up tight in their cases against the wall near the window.

"I can't explain this. They should be in their cases." He pointed to the right where the empty cases sat.

"They're super creepy." Her hand tightened around his. "What's going on?"

"I wish I knew. I..." He tried to offer a smile with what he was about to admit, but it wouldn't come. "I've always felt like something...something else is in the house with me. I've never seen anything, though. It just feels..."

"Evil," Mona whispered, finishing his sentence when he couldn't find the right word.

Evil worked perfectly.

Lifting her hand, kissing the back of it, he regretted it when she shivered. "I should've told you not to come back inside. You shouldn't be here."

Her brows furrowed low. "I can't leave you alone with... with...that thing. You could—" A smile touched her lips. "Well, you can't die, but who knows what would happen to you."

"I'm not worried about myself, Mona, but I'm worried about you. We have to get you out of here."

Her smile died as a fierce determination lit up her features. "I'm not going anywhere. We'll fight this evil spirit together."

"How?" His grip tightened. "I won't allow you to get hurt. You need to leave."

Mona waved a hand at the dolls. "You said they were in their cases before, but now they're not. Maybe..." She glanced at the cases against the wall, then back at the dolls lined up in a row. "Maybe the dolls are really dead people the malevolent spirit acquired."

Confused, he shook his head. "I don't understand."

"Maybe they came out of their cases to help you...us. Maybe they're trapped in the doll and need our help."

Mason looked at the dolls, going down the line, taking in each face with care. Their eyes all followed his path, watching him. The same way they had when he first walked through the door. Every time he moved, their eyes moved with him. Each doll had a smile on their face with their arms hanging loosely by their sides. It unnerved him more than he cared to admit.

He certainly would never admit it to Mona either.

He tore his gaze away and met Mona's eyes. She looked a lot calmer than she had out in the hallway, a whisper of a smile still shining on her beautiful face.

"They don't look friendly, Mona. I should've never picked this room to bring you in."

"Well, they do look creepy. I will admit that, but..." She glanced at them, then back to him. "I don't get an evil vibe from them like I did downstairs."

"What do you suggest we do then?"

The sweet, tentative smile she wore disappeared. "I think I need to do some research. I need to leave and find out why you died. Why did you come inside this house in the first place?"

Mason's heart started to pound like crazy.

It was always a question he wanted answered.

Mona was right in one aspect: she needed to leave.

She needed to stay away. Far away.

She wasn't safe here.

Lowering his mouth, he kissed her. The warmth he felt holding her in his arms didn't compare to the ecstasy as he gently pressed his lips against hers.

Before he could change his mind and cave in, he stepped away, his arm outstretched, barely hanging on to her hand.

"What are you doing, Mason?"

"Leave." His expression turned stern. "I don't want to see you again, Mona. Leave, and don't come back."

He let go of her hand.

OH HELL NO!

"MASON?" Mona glanced around the room with a frown. "You better come back here and hold my hand. We're not done talking."

A cool breeze touched her arm, but he didn't appear. Was that him?

Darting a glance at the dolls, a shiver raced down her spine. They hadn't moved, but their eyes, as if they were human, had widened into large saucers.

Mona took a step toward the door, almost tripping over Scatter. "Mason?"

Meow.

Looking down at Scatter, she nodded. "I agree. We should leave this room, especially if Mason is going to act like every other man that has entered my life. Like a complete douche."

Meooow.

"Oh hell no! I don't care what you say, Scatter. He just gave me a brush off." Rolling her eyes, she stalked to the door, ignoring the dolls' eyes that followed her every move.

"No ghost is giving me a brush off. He deserves every nasty name spit at him."

Yanking the door open, she waited for Scatter to exit as well, still refusing to look at the dolls. She might be upset at Mason for ignoring her, but the dolls creeped her out. Although, she had a strange feeling she was meant to save them. The people trapped inside. The souls that needed to be set free and...follow the light, maybe. She had no clue, but she'd find some answers soon.

She had a mission.

"Find your dumb master and tell him I'll be back." Mona eyed Scatter with a look that told him she meant business, then headed for the front door.

Swiping her jacket and snacks she dropped earlier, she didn't stick around to see if the evil spirit still lingered. She grabbed the doorknob. This time she got it open on the first try. Wiggle, then lift, just like Mason said.

She didn't even look at the house as she drove away. Because if she looked, she might falter in her determination. Her stomach gurgled with unease that she was making a colossal mistake leaving.

Mason was in danger.

But that's why she had to leave. She had to find answers.

By the time she made it to the library, she had devoured the bag of chips and ate a few gummy worms.

Waving to Bonny behind the front counter, she headed toward the back of the library where the microfilm reader sat lonely on a single desk.

She enjoyed coming to the library to check out books now and again. Rarely did she venture into this area, but she knew how it all worked.

After two hours of searching film after film, she finally

found something that made the chills she felt in the house pale in comparison.

Young Woman Vanishes Without a Trace

(St. Cloud Chronicle – February 19, 1968)

POLICE ARE ASKING for the public's assistance in locating a woman who went missing two days ago. Abigail Johnson, age 21, was last seen leaving her apartment heading for her job at the Laundromat. Her car was found a few blocks from her apartment, although no signs of foul play. She has light-brown hair, approximately 5'2" with green eyes. If you see, or know any information concerning her whereabouts, please contact the St. Cloud Police Department.

Second Woman Vanishes

(St. Cloud Chronicle – March 5, 1968)

TRACEY COLTON, age 22, was last seen March 2nd leaving her apartment for her morning class at the local college. Police have no leads at this time as to her whereabouts. Her parents indicated she would never run off and insist something terrible happened to her. When asked if this is related to Abigail Johnson's disappearance, the police denied a correlation and declined to further comment. Tracey has light-blonde hair, approximately 5'6" with blue eyes. If you see, or know any information concerning her whereabouts, please contact the St. Cloud Police Department.

. . .

MONA COULDN'T TEAR her eyes off the screen as she scrolled article after article. Twelve women disappeared. All vanished without a trace, no evidence, and no suggestion of foul play. It's as if they got ready for the day, left home, and disappeared before arriving to their destination. A small gasp left her mouth as she read the next article.

12 Women, 12 Disappearances, Police Say Not To Panic

(St. Cloud Chronicle – July 23, 1968)

SINCE FEBRUARY 17TH, twelve women, ranging from age twenty to age twenty-five, have disappeared without a trace. No eyewitnesses have come forward with any leads to point the police in any direction. The latest woman, Sally Howard, age 23, was last seen two days ago leaving her apartment for a late afternoon lunch with her mother. When questioned, the lead detective on the case, Detective Mason Stewart, refused to comment but said they are pursuing all avenues and not to panic. Sally Howard has light-brown hair, approximately 5'4" with hazel eyes. If you see, or know any information concerning her whereabouts, please contact the St. Cloud Police Department.

LEANING AWAY FROM THE SCREEN, rotating her neck and shoulders, Mona tried to brush off the terror threatening to swallow her whole. Mason was the lead detective on the disappearances of twelve women. There were twelve dolls back at the house. It didn't make any sense.

After getting paper and a pencil from Bonny, Mona wrote everything down in chronological order, starting with Abigail's disappearance—where she was last seen, the route she normally took to and from work, and any evidence or leads listed in the newspaper clippings. Then she went to the next victim, and so on, until she reached victim number twelve, Sally Howard. Three hours later, working with the limited research at her disposal, another terrifying shiver raced down her spine when she saw a common denominator.

All twelve women took the same route to their destination. All drove past the creepy-ass house she bought.

How did Mason die?

Her finger hovered over the button to continue scrolling.

Did she really want to find out?

"Of course, you do, Mona. He might be a..." Her breath hitched. "Okay, he's not a douche, but he did hurt my feelings. He was just looking out for me. Of course, he was."

Mona nodded to herself. The house was evil. Twelve women disappeared. He couldn't remember, but instinctively he knew she wasn't safe. He only shoved her away because he was protecting her.

Well, she had to protect him, too.

She continued scrolling through the articles.

Detective Mason Stewart Missing

(St. Cloud Chronicle – August 1, 1968)

Just a little over a week after the disappearance of Sally Howard, the latest woman to vanish, Detective Mason Stewart, the lead detective on the case, cannot be found. He was last seen leaving the precinct to head to an unknown location. Chief Bower would not comment further when asked if it was related to the other disappearances. Once again, the police are asking if you have seen, or know any information pertaining to his disappearance, contact them immediately.

SHUFFLING all of her papers together, she stood up and grabbed her purse.

She didn't know how he died.

She didn't know who was responsible for the disappearances.

But she knew the house held all the answers.

"I'm coming back, Mason." Her lips thinned into a tight line. "And I will not be ignored."

WHERE WAS SHE TO GO? OUT OF HIS SIGHT QUICKLY.

THE HARD GLARE on his face didn't waver as he stared at the door. Almost zoned out, he was staring so intently. Then a soft meow with a gentle brush against his leg had him glancing down where Scatter walked around his legs looking up at him.

"I know. She's not coming back. It's been almost six hours." He looked away, hating the disgust in Scatter's eyes.

A cat. Disgusted at him. That's how low his life had become. Not being a ghost. No way. Having a cat look at him with disdain—like he threw up a hairball and swallowed it again—was the lowest point of his life.

It was his own fault. He told her to leave. He let go of her hand. He turned his back on her.

But only to keep her safe.

He didn't know why he felt compelled to get her to leave and never come back. He had no idea why he thought what lay beyond this door held the answers.

Fifty long years he roamed this house.

Fifty long years he questioned why and how he might've died.

Fifty long years he passed this basement door.

And not once did he ever attempt to open it or walk through it.

Not once did he have the courage to do so.

Until now.

Kind of.

Another brush against his leg had him looking down at Scatter.

"Man up and walk through. Is that what you're saying?" He glanced away, shaking his head. "I'm trying here. But we both know what's down there isn't...safe."

Taking a step near the door, his hand hovered close, but he didn't attempt to touch it. He could feel the evil pulsating his way. It was like an energy band, strong and fierce, and with the slightest touch, it would pull you through and you'd never return. Never survive.

Snatching his hand away, he took a step back.

Meooow.

"I don't know if I can do it, Scatter. If I go through that door, you can't come with." He looked down. "I might not come back." A harsh groan filtered out. "And what if Mona comes back? What if I walk through that door and she returns? What if I don't come back and she searches the house? What if she tries to open this door? What then? She'll...she'll..."

It was right there. Right in the back of his mind, yet not. He couldn't quite find the right words to finish the sentence.

She'll...die. No. He wasn't sure she would.

She'll...disappear. That sounded a bit more right, but still off somehow.

His ear twitched, listening, when he heard a soft thud echo down the hallway. Twisting around, he stared down the long stretch.

It sounded like the front door closed.

Did Mona return?

Or was the malevolent spirit playing games with him again?

"We better check that out before we tackle this task." He smiled at Scatter, knowing quite well that he wasn't fooled.

This was nothing more than a stall tactic. He wasn't ready to breach the threshold of no return. Because deep in his gut, he knew that's what would happen. He'd never return.

He walked slowly down the hallway. Even if it was Mona, she wouldn't be able to see him. Why was he walking slowly, almost tiptoeing? It was kind of ridiculous how much caution he was taking. What could he say other than he was nervous to see her?

What could he possibly say to make up for the horrible way he'd treated her? He hurt her feelings, and that was the last thing he ever wanted to do.

"Mason? Are you here?"

Her sweet voice swirled his way.

She *was* back.

She wanted to talk to him. Maybe she didn't hate him as much as he thought she did.

Increasing the pep in his step, he turned the corner, walking quickly through another hallway that would lead him to the foyer.

Except, when he reached his destination, she wasn't there.

Standing still, listening intently, he couldn't make out any sounds. No footsteps. No sweet, amusing murmurings she loved to do. No calling of his name.

Odd.

Where was she to go? Out of his sight quickly. That

didn't make any sense. She didn't know he was near unless he touched her.

She called his name. He came. She shouldn't have moved from this spot.

Meow.

Glancing behind him to the hallway they just fled, he shook his head. "We would've seen her pass us. She didn't go that way."

Meow. Scatter looked up.

He followed his gaze up the staircase.

"No. Not that room."

The last room on the left.

Where twelve dolls stood lined in a row.

Their crazy eyes watching his every move.

He didn't know what was worse—the basement door he couldn't step through or the room upstairs with the creepy dolls.

Well, he knew the answer to that.

The basement door was far worse.

"After you, Scatter." He held out his hand for the cat to precede him.

Meow.

Scatter's expression said he still wasn't amused.

Chuckling, he took the lead, praying and hoping Mona didn't hate his guts. And that she'd understand completely when he told her he never wanted to see her again. This time with more conviction in his tone.

SMELLS LIKE CHOCOLATE

MONA STOOD in front of the dolls, her head tilted, contemplating. How could she save them, release their trapped souls or whatever?

"Is there like a spell or something? Can you ladies talk?" Her brow rose. "Or do you just stare creepily at people? Seriously, it's unnerving. If you want me to help, you should stop staring at me like you want to..." She shrugged. "Like you want to suck my soul out of me."

Nothing but silence answered. The dolls' eyes widened, but no words came out.

Well, what had she expected? Nothing had been easy since she stepped inside this crazy house, so why would it suddenly get easier now?

"Why are you looking all crazy again? Stop staring so hard at me." She snapped her fingers. "Or are you trying to tell me something? What are you trying to say?"

Maybe it was a riddle. But what did eyes widening indicate?

Coldness wrapped around her.

Glancing around, she didn't notice anything else in the room. Where had the coldness come from? Was that why their eyes grew large? The malevolent presence was in the room with her?

Or Mason.

"Who's there? Mason, is that you?"

She jumped in her spot when Mason appeared, his cold, frigid hand holding hers. Her eyes narrowed. "I'm mad at you."

"I know. It was necessary. You need to leave. You shouldn't have come back."

"But I found—"

"I don't care. You don't belong here, Mona. Okay, fine. We had a moment or two. But, honestly, it was nothing. You don't mean anything to me."

Her lips thinned into a tight line. She squeezed his hand like a vice grip just so he couldn't let go without warning this time. "I've had about enough of guys saying things they don't mean."

"I..." His eyes turned to the floor. "You have to leave, Mona."

"Because it's not safe. I know. This house holds all the answers. To the reason why twelve women disappeared." She inhaled deeply. "Just like you did."

His eyes met hers. "What are you talking about?"

She lifted the papers clutched in her other hand. "I did some digging in the library. You were investigating the disappearances of twelve women in the area. Shortly after the last disappearance, you disappeared as well. I couldn't find anything after that. Nothing about you or any of the women's bodies being found. It's as if you all...vanished."

"I don't..." He shook his head, his grip tightening. "I don't remember any of that."

"Maybe because the house doesn't want you to. But we have to figure this out. We have to help these women." She held out her hand with the papers dangling in the air toward the dolls.

Mason followed her gaze. "You think...you think the dolls are the women."

She giggled and rolled her eyes. "Well, it sounds silly when you say it like that. But, yeah. Like their souls are trapped inside or something."

His face went blank as he stared at her. His look confused her. She wasn't sure if she could take it if he told her to leave. It hurt every time he said it, even though she knew he was only saying it to keep her safe. Because this house wasn't safe. Whatever evil entity was here, it wanted to hurt her. And him.

Without warning, he pulled her closer, wrapping her in his icy embrace. "I can't see you get hurt. Please, Mona." His head tucked in between her shoulder and neck, his lips close, yet not touching her. "Please, Mona. I need you—"

"Don't say it," she whispered, cutting him off. "Just end your sentence there. Leave it at that. You need me."

His lips finally closed the distance. A cold, light kiss touched her neck. "Smells like chocolate. Why do you smell like chocolate? It makes me want to taste you everywhere."

Her breath hitched at his soft words. Oh, how she wanted him to devour her from head to toe. Press sweet, light kisses everywhere. Even if his touch was so cold and she felt like an icicle.

But he wasn't...real. He was a ghost. It didn't seem right to feel this way, to want him as she did.

When did she ever do what was right? She didn't.

"Let's solve this mystery and then you can kiss me wherever you want."

His hold on her tightened.

"Please, Mason. Don't tell me to leave. I have to help you."

He pressed another soft, chilling kiss to her neck. "There's this door..."

CATS AND DOLLS AND GHOSTS, OH MY

HOLDING MONA'S HAND TIGHTLY—MAYBE too tight—they headed downstairs and to the door he should stay far away from.

But even knowing her only a day—one day and it felt as if he'd known her all his life—he knew that Mona would not let this go. She'd keep digging and digging until she hurt herself. If he wasn't around to keep her safe, to make sure she didn't get hurt, another death would be on his conscience.

Not that he remembered those other women disappearing...dying.

But the truth was in the papers Mona held in her hand. He didn't solve their cases. He didn't find them and bring them home to their families. He didn't even find their bodies to bring closure to their families. So their deaths were on his conscience. And Mona's would not be added to that pile.

Here they were walking to the last place he wanted to go.

The hallway seemed to shrink the moment they took the first step toward the door.

Her hand wrapped securely in his started to burn hotter.

Too hot, where he was very tempted to let go; it seared his skin. By the sharp intake of breath next to him, she felt the same thing.

He should let go.

No!

He couldn't let go. He couldn't let her face this on her own, thinking he wasn't there for her.

Pushing the pain aside, he walked slowly with her toward the door, the hot, blazing pain getting more intense the closer they got.

"Cats and dolls and ghosts, oh my. Cats and dolls and ghosts, oh my. Cats and dolls and—"

He jerked to a stop, pulling Mona closer, his brows pleated together, his eyes filled with worry. She stopped muttering under her breath immediately.

"What are you singing?" he whispered, too afraid to speak normally so close to the door that held the realm of evil behind it.

A crooked, shaky smile touched her lips. "I don't know. Something to calm my nerves. It's a catchy tune, isn't it?" A shiver coated her skin, her entire body trembling.

"I'm hurting you."

Her lips twisted with pain, betraying the shake of her head that told him he wasn't, even though he truly was. "I'm fine."

His frown turned fierce, etched with the pain she refused to admit. "You're not fine. I'm hurting you. Because you're hurting me. Your hand is like I'm holding a hot coal, scorching my skin." He leaned closer. "But I can't let you go. I won't let you go through that door alone."

Her brows scrunched into confusion. "I'm burning you? That makes no sense. Your hand is so cold, it feels like my hand is stuck in a block of ice." She squeezed his hand hard. "And if you let go, I'll kill you."

A bright smile instantly lit up his face. "I'm already dead, my sweet Mona."

She matched his smile with one of her own. "You know what I meant. I was threatening you. Just take it. Nod and say, okay, Mona."

He nodded. "Okay, Mona."

Sweet laughter filled the small, dark hallway. He wanted to bottle up her laughter and save it for a rainy day when his loneliness would engulf him with such misery he'd wish he was more than dead. What was beyond death? He had to assume there was something if he was still stuck on earth in a creepy house filled with evil.

Because if they survived this, he never wanted her to come back to this house again. He'd miss her. He'd think of her every single day and every single minute of every single second of his life.

She pressed a quick, unexpected kiss to his lips, then started walking forward, tugging him along.

He couldn't hold back a wince and a low groan as the pain intensified so badly, he wanted to drop to his knees.

They stopped in front of the door.

"Mona..."

She met his strangled gaze, her face contorted with a throbbing pain as well. "We can do this. Just hold on tight, Mason. Don't let go. Whatever you do, don't let go."

He couldn't promise that. The pain was so intense, so brutal, he thought his hand was going to burst into flames at any moment. He couldn't even nod in agreement.

A moment of clarity hit him.

So fierce. So strong, he swore he saw stars dancing before his eyes, as if he were hit on the back of the head.

When they opened this door, he'd lose her forever. He'd disappear once again.

Blocking out the intense pain as much as he could, he wrapped her in his arms. It was like holding a ball of flame or stepping through a wall of fire, not even considering the consequences. Holding her so closely was burning him from head to toe.

And he didn't care.

Then he dipped his head and closed the distance, pressing his mouth against her soft, sweet lips. Not a tender kiss of good-bye. Not a simple peck to say he'd miss her. A hard, powerful kiss that said he'd remember her until he couldn't remember anything ever again, which was a high possibility. He must've walked through this door fifty years ago and forgot every single thing about what happened to him and the days and months leading up to his death.

He wouldn't remember her. It tore his heart into pieces thinking of losing the simple memory of her.

She opened her mouth, groaning in pain and pleasure, just like him. Their tongues met, danced, twirled, and said so many things that words would never be able to express.

One day.

He'd known this wonderful, lively woman one day.

It only took one day to fall in love with her.

Breaking the kiss abruptly, he took a step back, yet held her hand with a severe grip. He didn't wait for her to say anything. He placed his other hand on the handle of the door and opened it.

A deep, dark pit of blackness stared back at them.

Without thinking, without waiting, without offering any encouragement or words of love, he stepped through the door with Mona holding his hand in a vice grip. Nothing would break them apart.

Not even the bright flash of white light that stopped them in their tracks the moment they both stepped through.

It was so bright he couldn't even see Mona standing next to him, yet he felt her hand in his.

Then something tugged sharply on their grip.

Mona screamed.

The room plunged into darkness once again.

ALL THE VOICES

"MASON, DON'T LET GO!" She shouted it so loudly, she probably blew his eardrums and the person standing so close to them who was trying to tear them apart.

Except she couldn't see a thing. It was pitch black. First a bright white light, and now nothing but darkness.

It was unnerving. Even more so when she felt Mason's grip start to loosen.

"Mason!"

Why wasn't he answering her? She could feel his hand in hers, freezing her to the bone, but he said nothing.

Just as quickly as the tugging on their hands started, it stopped.

Silence surrounded them. Silence and darkness.

"Mason," Mona whispered, almost too afraid to speak.

She tugged on his hand herself when he still didn't respond. "Mason?"

Then a rushing sound echoed all around them. Like running water or something. She wasn't quite sure, but it was loud and deafening.

Neither of them moved. The sound intensified as each

second ticked by. She wasn't even sure Mason was with her anymore. She knew he was standing next to her, but she felt as if she had lost him somehow.

As quickly as the rushing sound appeared, it vanished.

Then voices started shouting. All at once, like a stereo blasting into a quiet room. What were they saying? She couldn't quite make it out. It sounded as if they were surrounded by a dozen or more people whispering viciously in their ear.

Yes, viciously.

Like they were upset.

Help us.

Or maybe frightened.

The dolls.

Well, not the dolls, but the women trapped inside. Were the women themselves surrounding them right now?

Don't stop.

Keep moving.

We need you.

Help us.

A loud, piercing scream erupted.

When Mason's grip tightened painfully, she realized she was the one screaming. The voices disappeared as soon as she stopped screaming.

"Mason, are you with me?"

She didn't mean physically. She had to know whether he had control of himself because, with his silence, she had to wonder if the evil force was doing something to him.

He squeezed her hand once.

Good.

He couldn't speak for some reason, but he could communicate.

"We have to keep going."

The creepy-ass dolls, or the women themselves, said so.

She started forward, but her arm jerked when she realized Mason wasn't following. Tugging on his hand, she whispered low, "We have to keep going. They need us."

He still wouldn't budge.

What was going on? Why was this happening? She wasn't too fond of walking in the pitch-black either, but she'd do whatever she had to do to help these women and Mason.

"Whatever's happening to you, fight it. Don't let the evil...the evil...asshole win."

It didn't sound threatening enough, calling the evil entity an asshole, but it was the best she could come up with. And it worked. It *was* an asshole hurting the man she loved.

Yes, she loved Mason. So much. With all of her heart.

What do you fight evil with?

Love. All the love.

Walking closer to Mason, she felt around in the dark, touching his chest, his neck, her hands gliding across his adorable beard until she covered his lips. Leaning closer, she replaced her hand with her lips, kissing him with all the passion and love she had inside.

Barely moving away, she whispered even lower than before, in case the evil asshole was listening, "Stay with me, Mason. Please, stay with me."

His hand tightened as his lips crashed down on hers again. A deep, searing kiss that told her everything she needed to know without words. He was here with her and he wasn't going anywhere.

She started to back up, forcing him to follow her as they kissed. They moved slowly, even though they kissed with passion. Mouths melding as one. Tongues clashing. Low moans and growls echoing in the deep darkness. She took the sign of Mason's sweet growls while they kissed as a good sign. He wasn't completely silent.

A cry of pain tore from her lips when she backed into a wall, her head smacking it hard. Mason's grip on her hand slackened. The strange tug from before came again, trying to rip them apart.

———

MASON TRIED to yell Mona's name, but no sound came out. It was frustrating as hell having no voice when everything around him, even the weird whispers from before, could speak. Why couldn't he?

He strengthened the grip on her hand, refusing to let whatever was tugging on them win. He cupped the back of Mona's head, rubbing, hoping she was okay after running into the wall. Pressing her closer, he found her lips once again with a sweet, slow kiss.

The burning pain, like his entire body was on fire, was almost too much to bear. But no matter what, he would never let her go. He'd go down in flames before he let her go.

Because that's what the evil entity wanted.

The tugging on their hands stopped once again. But he didn't stop kissing her. He didn't stop holding her in his arms.

Out of nowhere, the bright light returned. Unlike before, when he could see nothing before him when the light flashed, he could see Mona this time. The fear etched in her eyes scared him. But it also made him stronger, more determined to get her out of this alive.

"I won't let you get hurt." It barely came out in a whisper, his voice cracking and breaking. It didn't matter. His voice was coming back.

"I won't let you get hurt either."

He smiled, kissing her one more time. Then he stared at the wall behind them. Glancing from side to side, the wall looked as if it stretched on for miles. How was that possible? Where were they?

"Umm...Mason?"

"Yeah."

"Look behind you."

Turning around, Mona's hand still wrapped in his, his eyes rounded at the sight.

A spitting image of him stared back. It was uncanny. Unnerving. And so very odd.

"You finally came back."

His brows rose in confusion. He didn't know what to say...to himself? Was this the evil entity?

"Who are you?"

Geez, Mona was braver than him, asking this thing a question.

The man smiled, just as he would've. "I'm Mason. The part that remembers everything that happened. I've been stuck in this hellhole for..." He shrugged. "I'm not sure. It's dark all the time. This is the first time the light came back on."

He looked skeptically at his lookalike, his voice still cracking as he spoke. "How do you know I don't remember anything?"

"Because he told me. When I first walked in here, trying to find those missing women, he told me I was stuck here forever unless you, my other half, figured it out."

"Figured what out?"

"How to save us. How to fight the evil." He shrugged

again. "I don't know how to explain it. It's all...crazy to even think about."

"Tell us what happened," Mona said firmly, yet with a slight tremor in her voice.

He squeezed her hand in reassurance. He didn't know whether they could trust this thing yet, but he wouldn't let anyone, or anything, hurt her.

"I was trying to find the missing women. It led me to this house. They all passed it before they disappeared. Nobody lived here. It was abandoned, so I let myself in. I found the dolls upstairs. I should've walked out when their eyes looked at me, pleading. But I think it was the terror in their eyes that had me keep looking. When I walked into what I thought was the basement, that's when my hell started—when I disappeared just like them. Instead of my soul trapped in a doll, part of me was turned into you." He pointed at him as if it all made sense. But none of it did.

"Who is he?" Mona asked.

The thing shrugged. "Something powerful. The devil, maybe. I don't know. But he's able to turn this basement into whatever this place is. He told me you wouldn't have any memory, but if you could figure it out, we'd all be saved. He laughed like it was one big joke."

Mona's eyes narrowed. "So, we saved everyone? By walking in here? It sounds too easy. I don't trust you, buster. I don't care that you look just like Mason."

The thing chuckled, yet his eyes fell into despair. "I see why myself likes you. You're refreshing."

"I'm not you." Was he? Could this thing, the man who looked just like him, be telling the truth?

Or was it the devil trying to trick them? Before he disappeared, he would've never believed in such evil things, but living it, dealing with it for the past fifty years, oh, he believed. Could he trust this thing? Himself?

"We're one and the same. You're just the part of me that doesn't remember what happened. I honestly don't know how to solve this. I don't know how to save these women from hell, and that's all I wanted to do." The thing pinned his stare at Mona. "But I think you're the key. Stuck here, I couldn't see anything in the darkness, but I could hear you two. I heard everything. You're the key, Mona. You can save us."

"She's leaving here safely," he growled. Whether he was speaking to the devil or not, he wouldn't let anyone harm Mona.

"Love conquers all. It always does."

He whipped his gaze to Mona's whispered words. "What?"

She turned in his direction. "I love you, Mason. I think I understand."

His brows furrowed low. He didn't understand at all.

Before he could stop her, she moved forward, grabbing hold of the thing's hand, while still holding his.

She looked directly at the thing that claimed it was him and smiled. "I love you, Mason."

The thing smiled back.

Then the entire room burst into a bright light, all the voices screaming around them, even Mona, although he couldn't see her. But he felt her hand.

The intense burning pain in his hand didn't deter him. He wouldn't let go.

He did the only thing he could think of.

"I love you, Mona."

He swore he heard the thing say the same words at the same exact time.

IT DIDN'T WORK

MONA COULDN'T STOP SCREAMING from the pain in her hand as she held Mason's frozen hand and from the voices screaming in her ear. The bright white light was so vibrant she had to close her eyes. She couldn't see Mason anyway, so it didn't matter if she closed her eyes.

Among the cries of terror, she heard his voice.

I love you, Mona.

The second she heard it, the voices stopped screaming. The entire room went silent.

Her hand that should've been clutching Mason's hand was gripped in a tight fist, her fingernails digging into her palm.

Why wasn't he holding her hand? She didn't even feel him let go. It's as if he disappeared into thin air. Or was he still with her?

She was too scared to open her eyes. Although, she sensed the white light was gone and she was standing in the dark.

It didn't work.

If she was in the darkness, then what happened to Mason all those years ago must've just happened to her.

Oh, dear.

She was a ghost.

Wait.

"Don't panic, Mona." She let out a slow breath. "Open your eyes."

Right. All she had to do was open her eyes.

She could do this.

Slowly, almost painfully, she opened her eyes. It was dark like she had suspected. But not so dark that she felt lost in the deep abyss—whatever an abyss was. She really didn't know. And she was letting her mind wander instead of figuring out where Mason disappeared to.

"Focus, Mona."

He definitely wasn't in the room with her anymore.

Glancing around, trying to make anything out, her eyes slowly adjusted to the dark. She flinched when she saw the stairs. Walking carefully, afraid she might run into something, she made her way to the stairs.

Wait? Stairs?

Where had the stairs come from? Was she in the basement for real?

Screaming and jumping, she threw her hands above her head when something touched her face. Something that felt strangely like a piece of string. Like a string attached to a light.

Frantically swinging her hands in the air, she found the string and pulled hard on it.

The room filled with light.

She screamed again, backing up until she fell on the bottom step.

Slapping a hand over her mouth, hoping to hold in more

screams, she stared in horror at the large cases lined against the wall.

In each clear case, dressed in different colored dresses, were the twelve women who disappeared fifty years ago. Not dolls, like before, but the women themselves. She wasn't sure how it was possible, but they looked perfect. As if they had just died that day. Their eyes were open, staring wide-eyed and alert as if they were waiting for the brutal blow of death.

Thank you.

She shivered as the soft voice floated by her ear, almost like a cool breeze on a beautiful sunny day.

Breathing heavily, trying to calm her racing heart, she finally let go of her mouth and stood up. Taking a step up, she kept her gaze on the women, yet none of their eyes moved like the dolls had.

"I'll be right back." She giggled, half hysterically. "Well, not me. I'm calling the police. They'll be back. Or not back. Because they haven't been here yet. Well, that's not true. Mason was here. But he's not anymore. Do you ladies happen to know where he went?"

The women didn't move. Didn't flinch. Didn't blink. No weird whispers floated by her ear either.

"Silly question. You're all dead. So, yeah. I won't be back. But the police will come and do..." She waved her hand in the air. "You know, whatever police do. That thing. Evidence and crap. Okay. I'm going now."

She whipped around, a little too fast, nearly falling again on the steps, then raced up the stairs. The door to the basement stood wide open. She slammed the door shut as soon as she exited.

Meow.

She screamed again. Then she started laughing and

shaking her head at the dumb cat that sat in the hallway. "Damn it, Scatter. Not funny, scaring me."

Meow.

"I don't know where he is. But..." Her bottom lip trembled. "But I'd like to think he went towards the light. Like the women probably did. It's nice to know you're still around. You crazy-ass cat. I'm not even a cat lover."

Scatter jumped and Mona had no choice but to catch him. He immediately started purring in her arms. "Well, I guess I'm a cat person now. Damn you."

Before calling the police, Mona walked upstairs to check out the dolls. The room was empty, not a doll in sight. She continued checking the rest of the house for Mason and coming up empty. She called his name constantly, hoping against hope his cold, freezing hand would grab hers. It never did.

She finally called the police to report the bodies in her basement. It didn't take long for the cavalry to show up. Police of all kinds. Uniformed officers, detectives, even the chief of police himself.

Mona sat on the porch swing that didn't look like it'd support her weight, but it did, so she didn't move. She spoke when asked a question, but otherwise, she said nothing.

The chief of police explained her house would be a crime scene for a few days, maybe even a week—not surprising—and asked if she had somewhere else to stay. Of course not. She moved out of her apartment when she bought this crappy-ass house. But she nodded and said, "Yep." What else could she say?

After giving her contact information to him as well, he said she could go. Grabbing Scatter, who jumped in her arms immediately when she told him to come along, she headed for her car. She opened the door and he jumped out of her arms, situating himself in the passenger seat as if he'd done it a million times.

"You're a weird-ass cat." She smiled. "I have a feeling we're going to get along fabulously."

"I wouldn't doubt it. He loves you."

Mona screamed, jumping back into the car door hanging open.

Mason stood before her, a silly grin on his handsome face.

"Mason?" She reached out her hand, then snatched it back, afraid to touch him, to hope he was real. "Wait? I can see you. You're not touching me. How come I can see you?"

His sexy, silly grin broadened until she thought she'd faint from the glorious sight. "I have no idea. All I remember was saying I love you, and then I appeared in my house I used to live in. Needless to say, I scared the living crap out of the homeowner."

She poked him in the chest. He felt real all right. Real and alive. Not a ghost at all. But he felt real when he had been a ghost when he held her hand. She poked him again. Yep, real. But it didn't mean anything.

"How many times are you going to keep poking me?"

Cocking her head to the side, she twisted her lips into a grin. "Maybe a few more. I'm trying to figure things out here."

He smiled in return. "Let me know when you figure it out because I'm dumbfounded."

Instead of poking him again, she laid her hand on his chest. He felt real, warm, and his heart pounded in tune with hers. Fast and crazy and erratic.

"You feel warm. Not cold, like before."

"I have a heartbeat, too." He stepped closer, snaking an arm around her waist. "I'm alive, Mona. Because of you. I have no idea what happened in that house, but you saved me. You gave me a second chance at life. You're taking Scatter with, wherever you're going. Is there room for me?"

"Do you snore?"

His lips curled into a devious smile. "When I have too many drinks, maybe."

"Well, I guess I can handle that." She placed her other hand on his chest, smiling up at him. "I'm so glad you're here. With me. I love you."

"Oh, you have no idea how much I love you, my sweet Mona."

His lips met hers in the sweetest, warmest kiss.

Well, maybe buying that house wasn't such a bad thing after all.

She found a man she loved, and she solved not one, but twelve fifty-year-old cold cases.

She could pat herself on the back.

Go her!

TIME TO FIGHT MORE EVIL

Squinting her eyes, then cringing, she forced herself to keep going. She had to do this.

"This is disgusting. Look at that. Oh my. That one is terrible. No way. I don't believe that one. That one isn't bad. I could maybe handle that one."

"What—"

Screaming, jumping in her seat, she whipped around in her swivel chair, her heart pounding as Mason smiled at her with that sweet grin of his she loved.

His lips were pressed together as if he were trying hard not to laugh.

"You didn't scare me. I knew you were walking up behind me. I totally did." She smiled, hoping her heart would slow down soon.

His chest rumbled as laughter spilled out. "You screamed like a hyena. I didn't mean to scare you. You were mumbling to yourself." He stepped closer, grabbed her hands to make her stand, then pulled her into his arms. "I love when you talk to yourself." Then he glanced over her shoulder to her laptop screen. "What are you looking at?"

Mona kissed him before extracting herself from his embrace. The past two weeks, since they met and defeated an evil force, he loved to touch her. All the time. If she was near, he had a hand on her. She found it adorable, and she knew he needed it since he had lived for the past fifty years not being able to touch anything. Not even a simple object like a doorknob.

Sitting down, a tender smile touched her lips when a hand landed on her shoulder.

Oh, how his touch always electrified her.

She was also grateful his touch warmed her to the bone instead of turning her into an icicle.

"I'm researching." She tapped the screen. "We need to be armed with knowledge, otherwise we'll be walking into danger like two bumbling idiots."

"Walking...into danger..." His hand tightened on her shoulder. "You've lost me, my sweet Mona."

A giddy, loving sensation pulsated through her veins at his adoring endearment. He loved to call her 'my sweet Mona.' Her heart always did a little pitter-patter of excitement when he did.

Then she forced her mind to stay on track and hoped Mason didn't freak out.

She tapped the screen again. "I found us a job. Something we're good at. You know, since we're both...jobless."

His hot breath fanned her neck as he leaned closer. A soft kiss followed before a chuckle fell from his lips. "Bigfoot. A Hellhound. A...nuckelavee. What is a nuckelavee, and why do we care?"

Mona twirled around in her chair, offering a sympathetic smile, hoping to ease the blow. "It's a horse-like demon that causes havoc in Scotland. Obviously, I don't think we start right off the bat with something so difficult, but it's good to know what we're up against." She winced as she glanced at the screen. "Actually, we should skip all of those you mentioned. We should start simple. A low-level demon, maybe. A cranky ghost. You know, something manageable."

Mason grabbed her hands and made her stand, pressing a light kiss to her lips. "I don't know what you're talking about, but the only thing I want to manage is to figure out the remote control that has way too many buttons."

She cocked a brow. "Only I handle the remote control. Paws off, buster." Then she snatched a kiss. "We're going to fight the evil in the world. Someone has to fight the evil. And since we're experts, I figured we could start tomorrow. Or maybe the next day. We need to buy supplies. How about we start next week? A week is a good amount of time to prepare."

"Fight evil?" He laughed as he brushed a soft hand across her cheek. "I don't want you near anything resembling evil. I almost lost you."

"But you didn't. I didn't lose you either. We can do this."

"Mona, we're not experts. I was a ghost for the past fifty years. I need to catch up on modern-day technology, not fight monsters."

Meow.

Mason looked down at Scatter. "You're not a part of this conversation."

"Scatter has a point."

"He meowed. He didn't say anything important."

Mona tilted her head and grinned. "He agreed with me."

He kissed her again, more forcefully, as if he could persuade her with a kiss. "You didn't have lunch yet. We should get some food in you. You know how you get when you're hungry."

She did get cranky and a little crazy when she got hungry, but this wasn't hunger pains. She was being serious.

Patting his cheek, brushing her hand across his soft beard, she held her smile in place. "I'm being serious."

Then she slipped out of his embrace once again and grabbed a small brown, worn journal sitting near the laptop. "I found this digging through my mother's things. It explains why I've always been weird, the outcast in life."

A warm hand touched her shoulder. "You're far from weird, my sweet Mona. You're special. You're one of a kind. And I love you just the way you are."

She loved him. It had only been two weeks since they met, but she loved him as if they'd been together for fifty years, instead of him being stuck in a house, alone, as a ghost for fifty years. They had yet to be back to that creepy house, and she didn't think she'd ever step inside again. Mason agreed. He wasn't eager to go back there.

It's a good thing she didn't pay too much to purchase it. She did snag it for a deal. Now she knew why—because it housed the underworld of evil. The devil, perhaps. They still didn't know, and it wasn't something they talked about often.

Of course, she didn't think she'd be able to sell it. Since that crazy day, they'd been staying in a cheap motel, figuring out their finances—or more like, her finances, since Mason was supposed to be dead. They still hadn't decided where they were going to live.

If she had her way, they'd be on the road, fighting evil. Because, even though she thought she knew her mother, she didn't.

Her mother fought evil all her life, never once confessing. Although, the entries weren't entirely clear what kind of evil her mother fought. It would take her a while to decipher everything. There was a mixture of diary entries stemming from a day at the park with her to the description of a vampire.

"Don't you want to know what's in this journal?" She looked at him. "It has a nice entry about ghosts."

Mason looked quizzically as he eyed the journal. "You figured out how to help me on your own."

"Yeah, but this journal could help me more than just walking into the dark."

"What was your mother...I'm confused. I'm a detective, not...whatever you want to call this endeavor."

"You can still keep the title detective." She threw him a saucy smile. "I think it's sexy, calling you Detective Stewart."

An adorable grin punctured his handsome face. "Mona, I adore you." His grin vanished, just like those times he disappeared right before her eyes. "But we almost died. I can't see you get hurt."

"I've been lost in life for so many years, never fitting in. As soon as I touched this journal, I felt a powerful jolt hit me. I'm meant to do this. To save people." She placed a hand over his heart, savoring in the way it beat steadily, confirming he was truly alive. "I want to save people with you by my side."

"We don't know the first thing about this kind of stuff," he muttered as he threw his hand toward the computer screen.

"Which is why we need to brush up on our literature." She tapped the journal. "And visit my aunt. I didn't know I had an aunt."

Shaking his head as a silky smile graced his lips, he pulled her into his arms. "This is crazy. The past two weeks have been crazy. Meeting you was crazy. Being alive again is crazy."

"And I'm crazy. I get it."

"No, you're perfect." He kissed her. "And I'll do anything for you. Let's skip the nuckelavee for now. I don't want to deal with a demon or a devil-like creature so soon. Or Bigfoot. That sounds super dangerous. I mean, even a Hellhound doesn't sound safe."

"We can do this." Her face lit up. "And just think, when we do decide to defeat a nuckelavee, we get to travel to Scotland."

Laughter filled the room, then his lips were covering hers, telling her how much he loved her.

Oh, what fun they would have fighting evil.

Mona and Mason. Evil crime-fighters. Evil be gone. Evilinators.

Well, okay. She had to work on a good name to call them.

But they had a purpose in life now, and she couldn't wait to get started.

———

WITCH WAY TO TURN

A MONA & MASON MYSTERY - #2

A Special Note

Are you ready for another mystery with Mona and Mason? This story was once again written with help from the lovelies in my group (Love & Happy Endings). Every week they used to give me a writing prompt and I'd write my flash fiction. I haven't done that in a few years though. I started it around Halloween 2019. Every chapter title is the writing prompt that I had each week, except the last chapter, THE START OF A NEW PATH. It's a never before seen chapter! I sincerely hope you enjoy this latest Mona and Mason mystery!

Happy reading!
🩶 MUCH LOVE, AMANDA SIEGRIST

THE WATER'S BEEN TURNED OFF.
THERE'S A BROKEN PIPE.

HE DIDN'T THINK he'd ever get to take a shower again. It was one of those luxuries that he never contemplated losing. It was always there, a part of his routine. Get up, go to the bathroom, jump in the shower, brush his teeth, trim his beard, get dressed and out the door for work.

Until it wasn't.

Because he had been a ghost for fifty years.

But not anymore. He was a whole man, alive and well. He had a heartbeat again. He was able to take breath after breath, inhale and exhale. He got cold and hot, shivered and sweated. He could chew and swallow, get heartburn and belch. He could do everything.

He would never take anything for granted again. Not even a simple shower.

While he knew it drove her up the wall sometimes, he couldn't help but take a shower quite frequently. Some days, even two or three times a day. He always had a good excuse for taking one. Like, he just ran and was all sweaty. He didn't like to go to bed feeling dirty. He cleaned out the litter box and felt disgusting. That excuse was probably borderline ridiculous, but he used it a lot.

Stepping into the shower, he inhaled heartily, eager to feel the hot water hit his skin. Turning the knob, the wide smile on his face fell into a frown.

A few drops of water trickled out, but that was it.

Unacceptable. The water had to work.

Stepping out of the shower, he opened the bathroom door and went in search of the woman who could make his heart race with one delicate smile. That could make him laugh at the drop of a dime. That could skyrocket his anger with little effort.

His sweet Mona.

A startled scream echoed as he walked into the living room. His grin widened.

"Must you walk around the house butt naked. It gives a woman ideas."

Mason chuckled as he drew closer to Mona. He wrapped an arm around her waist. "Like?"

Her hands slid up his back in a gentle caress. "Like...use your imagination. Why are you naked?"

He felt like that had to be a rhetorical question. He told her he was going for a run, which meant he would automatically take a shower when he returned. And he just got home from his run not even five minutes ago.

Although, maybe she wanted more sex. That was another luxury he swore he'd never take for granted again.

Sex with Mona was to-die-for. Not that he wanted to die—again. Or become a ghost—again. But she always managed to make his heart pump faster, his skin tingle with bliss, and his desire soar without effort. Hell, he could take her right here and now in the living room. He never passed up an opportunity for sex.

"I wanted to take a shower and the water won't turn on."

Mona rolled her eyes and then glanced at the floor, shaking her head. He followed the direction of her gaze and groaned.

Scatter sat quietly next to her feet, staring up at them. Mason swore Scatter wore an annoyed look on his furry face. He loved that cat with his entire heart, but sometimes a man needed space and a moment alone with the woman he loved. Scatter didn't know boundaries—at all. They were always forced to close the bedroom door and lock it— because he was a smart cat—when they made love.

"Do you want to tell him, Scatter, or should I?"

Another groan slipped out. "I don't think I want to know. I just want a shower."

Mona finally turned her attention back to him, placing a light kiss to his lips. "You had one before you went running, which doesn't make sense to me when you insist on taking another one when you get back from running. It's a waste of water."

"I like showers."

"I know." Her soft expression said she understood why he liked them, yet her eyes held a bit of discipline as if she wanted to spank his ass for wasting water so much. Then she patted his butt cheek. "The water's been turned off. There's a broken pipe."

Well...that was unfortunate.

One, because he wouldn't be able to take a shower.

Two, because they were broke. Flat broke.

It had only been a month since Mona walked into his life and saved him. For the first two weeks, they rented a motel room. After that, they decided to rent a small house on the edge of town with the little savings she had left. It was rundown and falling apart, but it was dirt cheap and they had a roof over their heads until they figured out how to get him some credentials. He wanted to apply for a position in the police department. He wanted to be a detective. A real detective. Not the crime-fighting paranormal detective she kept insisting on.

"Let me get dressed and I'll fix the pipe."

Mona patted his ass again, which was not helping him one bit. He wanted to fix the busted pipe and take a shower. But every time she touched him like that, he wanted to carry her to the bedroom and show her how much he truly loved her.

Damn it. They didn't have time for that.

He needed a shower.

"Forget about the pipe. The water's off and it won't ruin anything. It'll be there when we get back."

He frowned. "Get back?"

She bit her bottom lip as her eyes lit up with pleasure. Both expressions were such a contradiction with each other. She appeared nervous, yet excited.

Which meant, whatever it was, he wouldn't like it.

"We're finally going to visit my aunt." The radiant smile that spread across her face made him want to smile.

But he didn't. He knew she was leaving something out, and as terrible as it was, he'd been trying to avoid visiting her aunt. Because he knew what would happen.

"And?" he said slowly.

"Andshehasacaseforustosolve."

This time he looked down at Scatter with a brow raised in confusion. "Did you make out what she said? Because it sounded a lot like gibberish."

Scatter meowed.

He rolled his eyes. Because it sounded like Scatter knew exactly what she said.

Mona's delicate hands grabbed his face, forcing him to look at her. "Scatter agrees this is a good plan."

A strangled laugh echoed between them. "I didn't hear a plan. I didn't understand anything you said."

She smoothed her hands across his beard, then up through his hair as her lips met his once more. "My aunt needs us. And I need answers."

"Needs us?"

Oh, this didn't sound good at all. He wanted to ignore what she was trying to tell him and take her to their bedroom and love her until she forgot everything she was about to say.

"I said that my aunt...has a...caseforustosolve."

That time, although she still strung her words way too close together, he understood what she said.

A case for them to solve.

And he knew it was not a case he would like.

"What kind of case?"

Her lips widened into a deep grin. "A nasty vampire. Exciting, right?"

Scatter meowed as if he agreed with Mona.

Exciting?

Hell, no.

But he couldn't let his sweet Mona go alone.

"I have a feeling I'm going to regret this."

WHAT IS THAT?

MONA GRABBED her suitcase filled to the brim with almost her entire closet and tossed it into the trunk. Next, in went her sleeping bag, tent, first-aid kit, and everything else she thought might be useful in hunting a vampire.

She had no idea. She had never sought one of those creatures out. Hell, a month ago she didn't think ghosts existed, and Mason was proof they did. But one could never be underprepared for such a thing as vampire hunting. A person could only be over-prepared.

"What is that?"

The low timbre of Mason's voice behind her made her insides tingle with awareness. It didn't take much from him. A warm hand on her back. A caress across her cheek. A sweet smile directed her way. And the way he always said, "My sweet Mona." It made her giddy with happiness and filled with desire.

She turned around and met his slightly irritated, yet concerned gaze. "What?"

He pointed at the items in the trunk. "What is all of that?

It looks like you're packing the entire house. We're just going to visit your aunt for a few days."

"And fight a vampire, don't forget."

A strangled moan escaped his lips. "How could I forget? It's all you've been talking about this morning. Your research on the internet has not been very clear. Some say to cut the head off. Others say to stab them through the heart. A few think throwing holy water and garlic salt all over the thing will vanquish it. We're walking into unknown territory here."

Stepping closer, she rubbed a hand across his bearded cheek and smiled when he closed his eyes as if savoring the touch. "My aunt will have the answers. She said she'd explain everything to me when we get there. The things my mother never bothered to tell me. Who I am. What I can do. I can't explain it, Mason, but for the first time, I feel like I'm on the right path. I'm hoping you'll be right there with me."

His eyes opened, then his hand snaked around her waist and pulled her snug against him. "I'm never leaving your side. Never. If you're hunting vampires, then so am I."

Then a gentle kiss touched her lips. It wasn't long, but it was enough to tell her how much he loved her and would always support her.

"Let's hit the road so we reach her house before nightfall," Mason said, then swatted her butt with a wicked smile. "I'm driving."

"And if we get pulled over?"

"I'm driving." The firm look on his face said she wasn't going to win this battle.

Since Mason didn't have a driver's license yet, she always drove everywhere. He was technically dead in the record books, considering he disappeared over fifty years ago. They still hadn't gotten him documents so he could start living a normal life, like a normal human living being.

Mason loved to tease that she was a terrible driver. So, maybe she got a little aggressive at times. She would definitely not classify herself as a reckless, road-rage kind of driver. She just couldn't stand idiot drivers and vocalized it quite often.

"Keys?" He held out his hand, his eyes portraying he wasn't going to accept the word no. That he'd wrestle her to the ground and take the keys if he had to. She honestly wasn't opposed to the idea.

But they had things to do. A vampire to kill. Answers to get about her life and who she was.

"Don't get pulled over. Go the speed limit and don't drive crazy," she said with a stern tone of voice as she handed over the keys.

Mason chuckled. "Right. So, don't drive like you. Got it." Then he hollered over his shoulder, "Move it or lose it, Scatter! We're leaving."

He opened the back door and tossed in a small duffle bag and shut the door after Scatter zoomed inside.

She shut the trunk, not surprised he only packed a light bag. He didn't own anything when she met him, and what he owned now, she purchased for him. But they had everything they needed. She was prepared.

Buckling in, she braced herself, since this was Mason's first time driving in a very long time, and said a small prayer they made it to her aunt's house in one piece. It was a four-hour drive. Could he handle a drive that long? Did he even remember how to drive?

Mason started the car, shifted it into gear, then pressed the gas pedal. The car took off at a normal pace and he turned onto the road as if he hadn't spent the last fifty years as a spiritual being stuck in a haunted, cursed house.

"Just like riding a bike, my sweet Mona," he said as he grabbed her hand and kissed it. "It feels good to be behind the wheel."

"Well, you're doing good so far, but two hands on the wheel, buster. Let's not be too cocky." Then she took her hand back and arched a brow.

He complied and smoothly drove to their destination. The traffic was decent and not overly heavy for the first two hours. Once they hit the backroads, the traffic was light, almost non-existent. Her aunt lived up north. She had a nice house nestled deep in the woods a few miles out of town.

The sun was starting to dip below the horizon when they pulled into her aunt's unpaved driveway. A one-story house with a screened wraparound porch that looked dark and uninviting sat before them. The weeds around the porch were tall as if her aunt hadn't touched the garden in years. The lawn didn't look much better. No lights were on inside.

"She knew we were coming today, right?" Mason asked.

Mona nodded, then leaned forward in her seat as if that would give her a better view of the darkness lingering behind the closed door. The hair on her arms started to prickle and rise.

A tiny meow echoed behind her.

So, she wasn't the only one sensing something was wrong. Scatter felt it, too.

"Mona?"

Tearing her gaze off the house, she looked at Mason. "I've been calling her since I found the journal. She finally answered this morning. I don't know why she ignored me for so long, and when I tried to ask, she brushed me off. But she said she'd tell me everything my mother should've. Then she told me she needed me. It sounded urgent." Her gaze drifted back toward the house. "Why does it always have to be a creepy house?"

"I'm sure everything is okay. She probably left for some reason." Mason grabbed her hand and squeezed. "Let's make sure she's not inside. Maybe she's taking a nap."

Mona didn't believe that, but Mason was right. They had to find out if she was home or not.

They exited the vehicle. Mason took her hand as soon as they met in front of the car and made their way up the dirt path leading to the front door.

The screen door creaked when Mona opened it.

Her heart dropped, bursting with pain when she saw the splintered wood scattered all around the floor, the door itself hanging on its hinges.

"Well, that's not a good sign," Mason muttered.

No, it wasn't. But Mona came prepared. She refused to let another creepy house try to scare her.

"Let me go grab the stakes and ax from the trunk."

Mona tried to twist around, but Mason stopped her. The expression on his face was adorable with confusion and irritation mixed together.

"Stakes? Ax?"

Patting his bearded cheek, she smiled. "Vampires, remember? And we're not sure what kills one, so we stab them in the heart with the stake and then chop their head off. I also sprinkled holy water and garlic over all of it. Easy-peasy."

I WANT LICORICE

MASON SQUEEZED Mona's hand before heading back toward the vehicle. The sun was setting faster than he anticipated. Or maybe they stood staring at the broken door longer than they realized, but the night was almost upon them.

He unlocked the trunk and chuckled when Mona dug through one of the many bags she packed and handed him a flashlight.

Then, with an adorable grin, she held up an ax and what looked like a chair leg make-shifted into a stake.

He had taken a look at the broken pipe while she packed her bags, but he hadn't realized she made stakes out of one of their chairs. The end of it looked roughly sharpened. Pointy, but not *that* pointy, where it concerned him. Would it even penetrate skin?

"Well, which one do you want?"

Mason suppressed a groan, then grabbed the stake. He didn't want Mona to get hurt trying to stab a vampire with a dull stake.

"This is a terrible idea," he muttered as Mona continued to dig inside her bags.

"I don't see anyone else around to help my aunt." She paused, a tiny shiver touching her body. "If she's even alive. We should've left right away."

Placing a hand on her shoulder, he squeezed. "We'll find her. Let's not think the worst."

She nodded, then continued her search for whatever it was she was looking for. Mason had no clue. She had her ax and a flashlight ready to go; he didn't know what else she could possibly need.

"Ugh. Where is it?" Mona started tossing things out of one bag, making a mess. Pens, a notebook, several different kinds of granola bars, and a few pairs of shorts were tossed around the trunk.

He chuckled at her random way of packing things.

"Maybe I can help," Mason said, glancing around as he did. The sun was barely peeking through the tree line. He turned on his flashlight—a small, circular light that made him feel marginally better. The darkness, added in with walking into the unknown, had him nervous.

"I want licorice. I know I packed some. I have to find it."

Or maybe he couldn't help. He didn't know her method in packing, and although it looked random, he figured Mona had a system.

And yes. She needed to find her licorice. When she was hungry, she became crazy until she got something in her stomach. They brought snacks with for the ride, and she munched the entire way, so he knew she wasn't hungry. She probably needed the licorice to calm herself down.

Mona was a stress eater. They always had chips and candy stocked in the pantry for her to munch on every time something increased her anxiety. Which was usually the times she attempted to call her aunt and received no answer.

"Found it!" Mona stood up with a huge smile and a bag of red licorice in her hand.

She grabbed a few pieces out of the bag, shoved three into her pocket, and put one in her mouth. With half of it dangling out of her mouth, she grabbed her ax and flashlight and mumbled, "Let's slice and dice."

In all reality, her aunt was probably dead inside the dark, silent house. Nothing was funny about that. But with Mona, never knowing what she might say or do, Mason couldn't hold in his laughter.

"I'll take the lead." Mason headed back toward the house with the light from his flashlight leading the way and the stake ready in his hand.

He sure in the hell hoped he didn't have to use it.

Mona followed closely behind, soft chewing sounds echoing around them.

Scatter also trailed along, although quietly. He hadn't meowed or voiced his opinion since they arrived. Mason wasn't sure if that was a good thing or not because Scatter loved to interject his opinion on everything. And Mona always talked to him as if she understood him. Of course, so did he. He couldn't help it. As strange as it might seem, he could decipher one meow from another. He understood Scatter as if he were talking in English.

His steps slowed when he got close to the door, but he didn't hesitate or stop. Shoving the door open with his foot, loud scraping sounds scratched the floor. He stepped inside and swung his flashlight back and forth, taking everything in.

A small living room sat to the right with an old-fashioned boxed TV sitting on the floor and a drab green couch in the middle of the room. Everything was nice and tidy. No knick-knacks. No pictures on the wall.

To his left was the dining room. A simple table with six chairs and an old-looking China cabinet in the corner. Nothing sat on top of the table. In the cabinet, he could make out what looked like bowls and plates. Stepping farther into the dining room, he lifted his flashlight higher, making another sweep back and forth to catch a look into the kitchen. All the countertops were clean and clutter-free.

No sign of her aunt yet.

"Where is she?" Mona mumbled, obviously still chewing on the same piece of licorice. Or maybe she grabbed a new one.

"Let's check the rest of the place." Mason headed for the hallway and stopped when he came to a T. Two doors sat on his left, with one door to his right. All of the doors were shut tight.

"Divide and conquer."

Turning, he cocked a brow at Mona. "We stick together at all times. No negotiation."

A tiny meow answered.

"See. Scatter agrees." Mason waited for Mona to argue.

Except she didn't. She grabbed a new piece of licorice, put the end into her mouth, and grinned. "Fine. But you two won't be calling all the shots all the time."

He turned back to the task at hand and muttered under his breath, "We'll see about that." Then he turned left and opened the first door. There was a large bed in the middle of the room and a dresser near the window. The closet doors were closed. Mason peeked inside. Shirts, pants, and a variety of dresses were hanging in a color-coded order. Anything red started to the left and ended with things purple to the right. Organized like the color of a rainbow. The room was very neat and tidy.

The other room also held another bed and a dresser and a small desk in the corner. No clothes hung in the closet.

They ventured to the other side to check out the last room, which happened to be a bathroom. Clean and tidy.

"I don't understand," Mona said, as she swallowed the last part of her licorice. "Where is she? Why is the door busted but nothing else in the house looks disturbed?"

Mason shrugged, yet the hair on his arms prickled with unease. "I wish I had an answer."

They both jumped when a door slammed.

"I hate it when doors do that," Mona said with annoyance as she lifted her ax. "You're messing with the wrong woman, Mr. Vampire Man...or Woman. It could totally be a female vampire."

God, he loved his sweet Mona.

But that unease increased to intense fear when a low growl echoed down the hallway.

GOOSE BUMPS

"WE GOT THIS," Mona whispered as another low growl pierced the quiet, sounding as if it were inching closer.

She felt Mason tense next to her, then acted like her hero—which he was—and stepped in front of her.

"Stay behind me."

She didn't particularly like that idea because she didn't want him to get hurt, but sometimes it was easier not to argue with him. Of course, arguing with him was fun. She enjoyed it, especially when he scrunched his face in irritation, his eyes sparkling with annoyance as if he wanted to spank her. But right now wasn't the time to argue. They had no idea what was coming down the hallway.

Did vampires growl? She didn't think so. That sounded more like a werewolf, not a vampire. Were they dealing with a werewolf instead?

Ugh. Where was her aunt?

Mona grabbed the back of Mason's shirt as he slowly walked forward. The ax in her hand was heavy, but she was prepared to use it. Her swing wasn't the best. Every time she was forced to play sports at school, she was always the last person picked for teams. Nobody wanted an uncoordinated, accident-prone, bumbling idiot on their team.

Yeah, hopefully, she swung the ax with a decent aim.

Mason stopped at the corner, his entire body rigid.

Her arms tingled with fear.

Goose bumps.

Everywhere.

She shivered, trying to force the terror away. They could do this. There was nothing to be afraid of.

"Oh, for goodness sakes. Mona, come out."

She jumped at the sound of the old, crackly voice of a woman.

The werewolf—maybe—growled again.

"Stop it, Bozo," the woman chastised. "I don't have all day, child. Come out."

Mason turned around and cocked a brow, silently asking if they should listen to this crazy woman.

Mona shrugged. She had no idea who the woman was. It didn't sound like her aunt, but she hadn't talked to her that long on the phone. It had been a very brief call. "*I need you. There are some vampires we need to kill. I'll explain everything when you get here.*" Then her aunt rattled off her address and hung up. She didn't even wait for Mona to speak. Not once did she hear any crackle in her voice.

The woman behind the corner sounded much older and like someone who smoked a lot.

Mona glanced down when Scatter rubbed against her leg. His eyes pierced her with a direct stare as if telling her it would be okay.

Letting go of Mason's shirt, she smiled and then stepped around him and started to turn the corner before he could stop her. He followed quickly, grabbing her hand.

The lights turned on right before she turned the corner.

An older woman with white hair piled high on her head in a messy bun stood about five feet away with what looked like a wolf sitting by her feet. The wolf was all black, his eyes glowing green, staring hungrily at them, his lips curled into a snarl as if waiting to pounce and devour them.

They all stared at each other in silence, sizing each other up. The longer Mona looked the woman up and down from her colorful rainbow skirt to her plain orange shirt and the intensity in her eyes, she knew.

This was her aunt.

She couldn't explain why she didn't recognize her voice, but this woman had to be her aunt. She looked like her mother, just an older version.

"You look like your mother," her aunt Marcella said with a rasp.

"I was thinking you looked like her, too." Mona smiled.

Marcella scoffed, looking as if she wanted to spit and make her take back the statement. "What took you so long?"

"It's a long drive. We came as fast as we could." Mona pointed toward the front door. "What happened?"

Marcella glanced behind her shoulder, then laughed as if Mona had asked the dumbest question ever. "I had to test how long it would take to break down a door. A little too long for my tastes." Then she looked at Mason and nodded. "You look strong. Help me put this new door up and see how long it takes you to bust it down."

"Excuse me?" Mason asked.

Mona was just as confused. Why was her aunt trying to figure out how long it would take to bust down a door?

"Are you here to help kill these vamps or what?" Marcella propped a hand to her hip and tilted her head. The wolf tensed, growling.

Scatter meowed, stepping in front of her.

Mason looked down at Scatter, then at her aunt and the wolf. "Is he going to attack? Because I'd hate to have to hurt your...pet, or whatever it is. He keeps growling at us."

Her aunt patted the wolf's head as a short laugh escaped. "Bozo is a good boy. He doesn't attack unless it's necessary. And he's a wolf. A smart one. Just as smart as your...pet."

A short meow answered.

Marcella nodded at Scatter. "It's nice to meet you, Scatter. Why don't you and Bozo go have a snack while we finish this conversation."

To Mona's—and Mason's—surprise, Bozo turned around and started walking down the hallway. Scatter followed.

"What..." Mona started to say, but she had no words. She didn't know how to finish her sentence.

"There's much to talk about, Mona, but not right now. There's a nest of vampires in my woods and I want them gone. We can't attack without a plan. We need to time this down to the last second, which is why I need to know how long it takes to bust down a door."

"So, you honestly broke your door? I thought you were dead!" she shouted, taking a step forward. Mason's hand holding hers stopped her from approaching her aunt any closer. Which was a good thing. The anger building inside said she was liable to do anything.

How could her aunt scare her like that?

"Oh, it takes a lot to kill this witch." Then her aunt winked, turned around, and waved her hand for them to follow.

Mason squeezed her hand hard. She wasn't sure whether it was to stop her from following her aunt, or to give her the strength she needed to actually follow her aunt.

"Did she mean witch literally?" Mason asked with a crooked grin, although his brows were puckered low. "Like, a witch? An actual real witch?"

Raising her hand that held the ax, she rubbed his bearded cheek, albeit a bit awkwardly. He leaned into her touch. "I have no witchy clue."

But if her aunt was a real witch...

What did that make her?

WHY IS IT COLD AGAIN?

Mason held Mona's hand as they followed her aunt to the kitchen. The woman was a bit...odd. He wasn't sure what to make of her yet, but breaking down your own door seemed silly. There had to be a better way inside the vampires' domain without attracting all that attention. Sometimes, stealth was called for.

Especially since he had never come face-to-face with a vampire before.

Mason smiled as Mona's aunt pushed a mug toward him with what looked like coffee. He hoped so. She poured it out of a coffee pot. But since the moment she uttered the word witch, a strange tingling sensation had warped his body.

Marcella arched a brow, maintaining eye contact with him as she poured some coffee into a mug in front of Mona. The look unnerved him. It was as if she knew what he was thinking.

"Go on. It's only coffee." Then a twisted smile splayed across her lips as she picked up her mug and took a sip.

Well, it had to be safe. She poured it all out of the same pot.

Mason inclined his head and took a sip. Yep. Coffee. He was losing his mind, thinking the worst about Mona's aunt. She wasn't out to hurt them.

Although, the sinister smile still spread across her lips had him doubting himself.

Could they trust her?

He shivered as an odd blast of cold air hit his back.

"So, this isn't awkward," Mona mumbled as she looked between him and her aunt.

"He doesn't trust me." Marcella tilted her head as she gazed at Mona. "Do you?"

Mona shrugged. "You're family."

"Yet not quite an answer to my question. It doesn't matter." Marcella waved her hand absently in the air. "We'll take care of these vampires, I'll answer a few questions, and then you can be on your way."

Harsh.

It's as if her aunt didn't want to maintain any sort of relationship between them. She was only using them to defeat some vampires. Mona deserved better. She deserved everything.

"How many are there?" he asked, getting straight to the point. The faster he got Mona away from this woman, the better.

Another tremble touched his body as more cold air hit him.

Was the air conditioning on? What the hell?

"Four. I can handle two on my own, but not four." Marcella inclined her head toward the front hallway. "You'll fix my door and then see how fast you can break the next one down."

So demanding. She didn't even ask him. Only Mona was allowed to boss him around.

"I'll fix your door. But I won't be breaking one for you. How about I just pick the lock and we enter silently. The element of surprise would work better."

Marcella inhaled and exhaled slowly as she eyed him funnily. "Sadly, I don't know how to pick a lock. But you do?"

Mason nodded.

But if she was a witch...

"Why don't you just cast a spell or something?"

Mona sucked in a sharp breath at his sudden question.

Marcella smiled and then let loose a short cackle. "You have much to learn, my boy. Why don't you go take that shower you've been dying to have."

Mason flinched. How had she known? What kind of witch was she?

Although, a shower did sound nice.

She cleared her throat, her eyes narrowing. "It wasn't a request. I'd like to speak to my niece in private."

A warm, tender hand landed on his. He hadn't realized he had been gripping the countertop in a death-like grip. The moment Mona touched him, he relaxed somewhat.

"It's okay, Mason. I'd like to talk to her. You have been dying for a shower."

He pulled Mona into his arms and held her tightly, brushing his lips to her ear. "I don't trust her. You shouldn't either. And how did she know I wasn't able to shower this morning?"

Mona squeezed him back, holding on as if she never wanted to let go. "That's why I need to talk to her. I'll be fine."

He kissed her, then sent a dangerous glare at Marcella, warning her with one simple look that if she harmed Mona in any way, she'd answer to him.

Marcella bowed her head slightly, indicating she understood.

God, the woman was so strange.

He left the room and headed toward the bathroom. He'd let them think he was going to take a shower. But he wasn't. He had to be ready for anything.

It was tempting, though.

Turning on the water so they wouldn't suspect he was just sitting here waiting, he turned the faucet to the hottest setting. He needed to feel some warmth, at least.

His hand soaked up the warmth from the water as, yet again, cold air hit his neck.

"Why is it cold again?" he muttered as he glanced around the bathroom.

Everything appeared normal. Nothing out of place.

Why did he keep feeling cold air every so often?

A low scratch sounded on the door.

Mason wiped his wet hand on the towel hanging on the wall and opened the door. Scatter meowed softly and walked inside the bathroom. Before he could shut the door, the large wolf followed.

Taking a few steps back, he eyed the animal, wondering whether he could trust him or not. Because he didn't trust his master.

"Bozo, was it? How you doing, buddy? Friends?" Mason said tentatively, holding out his hand for the wolf to sniff and decide for himself.

The wolf inched closer, eyeing him. After a few seconds, he started rubbing his nose against his hand, as if saying he wanted him to pet him.

Mason crouched down and gave the wolf what he wanted.

"I wish you could tell me all about Marcella. Can we

trust her?" Because, oddly enough, he trusted Bozo. And he was a wolf.

Bozo nudged his hand to keep petting him as a low growl echoed in the tiny bathroom.

Mason wasn't sure how to decipher that.

Was Marcella friend or foe?

SHE IS DEFINITELY SNEAKY

"So, how did you know Mason wanted a shower?" Mona figured asking an easy question—was that an easy question?—would be better than jumping into questions about her mother.

She was dying to ask every question under the sun about her mother. Why she kept such secrets from her, why she never knew she had an aunt, and most importantly, who—what—was she?

Her aunt took a sip of coffee, contemplation on her face. Or, at least, the look of contemplation. Mona had no idea if her aunt was faking any sort of emotion. She didn't think they could trust her. Obviously, Mason had the same feeling. She wasn't about to ignore either of their feelings.

"Just an intuition," Marcella finally replied.

Liar!

Mona shivered as a rush of cold air hit her at the same time the harsh whispered word floated near her ear.

"Are you okay, Mona?" her aunt asked, standing up taller as she glanced around the kitchen.

Mona forced herself not to glance around as well.

Someone—or something—had whispered in her ear. Had her aunt heard it, too? Did she sense something?

What she did know was she trusted the unknown whisperer more than she trusted her aunt right now. Odd, when she had been looking forward to meeting her aunt since she found the journal.

"I'm fine. I'm just so curious about so many things."

Her aunt waved a frivolous hand in the air. "We'll have time to talk once we vanquish these vampires. That's our number-one priority right now." Then her eyebrows drew low as did her voice. "I'm worried about Mason, though."

The hairs on Mona's arms prickled with unease. "Why?"

Tilting her head with a concerned frown, her aunt said, "He's been through so much lately. I don't know if he can handle this. You don't know why he came back as a human. There are so many unanswered questions."

Mona took a small step away from the counter. She barely talked to her aunt on the phone. She had left dozens of messages for her to call her back, but she had never told her anything about Mason, especially the fact he had once been a ghost.

"How do you know all of that?"

A smile graced her aunt's face. Probably meant to look sweet and innocent, but Mona saw the sinister evil hidden beneath it. *She is definitely sneaky.* Mona forced herself to keep the comment inside, although she was so tempted to blurt it out like she tended to do so often.

"I know many things, Mona. In due time, I will explain. Mason needs to stay back, though. Between you and I, we can beat these vampires."

"I don't know how to pick a lock. You said you don't either."

"We'll worry about that later. We should go."

Mona glanced around, regretting the fact she urged Mason to leave the room. "I'm not leaving without Mason."

"I see things, Mona." Marcella frowned. "It doesn't end well for him if he comes with."

"What do you mean?" No, that wasn't right. She couldn't lose Mason. Not when she just found him.

"Quite simply, he'll die."

Her aunt said it so matter-of-factly as if she were reciting a dull news report instead of impending doom.

How would he die? By the hands of vampires...or her? Was she threatening Mason?

Marcella waved her hand toward the back door. "Come, child. We must go."

Mona glanced toward the hallway where Mason had ventured. Then she looked at her aunt. So many turbulent thoughts flooded her mind. So many worries. So many questions. She had no idea what to do.

Don't.

Another blast of cold air hit her as another whispered word accompanied it.

Her aunt's face morphed into rage. "I said let's go, Mona."

Yep, she was going to listen to an odd whispering voice rather than an aunt she thought she could trust.

Mona took a step backward.

"This won't end well for either of you if you don't listen to me."

Mona had to disagree. She didn't think it would end well *if* she listened to her.

"I fought the devil...I think," Mona said with a chuckle and a shrug. She still wasn't sure what she and Mason had defeated. "I'm not afraid to fight a witch...if that's what you really are."

Marcella cackled. A very witchy cackle, if Mona did say so herself. "I didn't want it to come to this."

A low growl sounded behind Mona. Turning her head, an eye on her aunt still, she saw Bozo, the wolf, standing a few feet behind her, the hair on his back spiked and his mouth opened in a snarl.

She was about to be mauled by a wolf.

Well, she wouldn't go down without a fight. She still had her trusty ax in her hand. Gripping the handle tighter, she dug inside her pocket and extracted a piece of licorice and took a bite.

Darting a glance between Bozo and Marcella, she took another bite of licorice but kept it between her lips as she raised the ax. "Let's do this."

WHY IS THAT CAT SCREAMING?

MASON STEPPED around the corner as Mona said, "Let's do this." She had a piece of licorice dangling in her mouth and the ax poised and ready for action.

Bozo growled again, low and menacing.

He patted him on the back as he winked at Mona and then glared at her aunt.

"I think Bozo wants you to stand down, Marcella. He and I had a great chat in the bathroom. He's not liking your attitude."

Mona shifted closer to him, the ax slowly lowering as she looked at her aunt. "Yeah, what he said."

It wasn't a time for chuckling, but his sweet Mona could always manage to make him find the humor in any situation.

"Bozo, come here," Marcella snapped, the fury intensifying in her eyes that appeared to glow a deep, dark red.

Bozo answered by growling and snapping in her direction.

Mason patted him again, thanking him for the protection. For choosing their side. He shivered as another brush of cold air swept across his skin.

Mona quickly glanced around, her brows puckered, and immediately raised her ax once again.

Had she felt the cold air, too?

What the hell was going on?

"We're going to go now." Mona started to back up closer toward him. "We're taking Bozo. Don't follow or we'll...you know, get scary with you. You don't want to mess with us."

Mason coughed to hide the laughter that wanted to escape. Oh, he loved this woman.

"Yeah, what she said." Then he backed up a few steps and glanced down the hall. "Scatter, let's go."

"If you think I'm just going to let you walk out of here, you're wrong," Marcella replied as she started to walk around the counter.

"If you think we won't fight back, you're wrong," Mason retorted.

Marcella suddenly let loose a sharp scream and jumped. Another loud screech could be heard in between her screams. Mason didn't realize it was Scatter meowing and hanging on her back until Marcella twisted around in a frantic circle, obviously trying to get Scatter off.

"Why is that cat screaming? What is Scatter doing? Is he okay?" Mona said with panic lacing her tone.

Mason grabbed her hand before she could rush toward Scatter and Marcella and pulled her toward the door. "We need to go."

"But...but Scatter. We can't leave him, Mason."

"He'll be along shortly." Mason shoved the busted door to the side, hoping he was right. He didn't even understand why Scatter didn't follow him and Bozo to the kitchen, or how he got behind Marcella to attack. He never saw him walk by.

Mason opened Mona's door, practically pushing her inside the vehicle, and raced to his side. Bozo jumped inside and he slid in right after.

"You can't leave without him." Mona grabbed his arm and gripped it tightly, her eyes round with terror.

"I won't." Then he flipped on the lights and started to back out of the driveway.

"What are you doing? This is the exact opposite of not leaving him," Mona yelled.

"Trust me, my sweet Mona," he whispered as he turned the wheel at the end of the driveway and then stepped on the brakes. Rolling down the window, he smiled when he saw Scatter sprint down the driveway.

Scatter leapt through the window, and Mason pushed hard on the gas pedal, barely parked for five-seconds.

He rolled his window back up.

The creepy old house with, what he could only assume was an evil witch, soon became nothing but a dot in the distance.

"Well, that was...not what I expected."

Mason darted a glance at Mona, hating the pain in her voice. He knew she wanted answers, especially since she found her mother's journal, and it didn't appear she'd be getting them any time soon—if ever.

Her aunt couldn't be trusted. If he had to guess, she lured Mona out here to kill her—him as well. Her aunt obviously didn't count on Scatter or her own wolf turning on her.

Scatter sat in Mona's lap while Bozo sat between them in the front seat. He wouldn't feel better until they put a lot of distance between them and her crazy aunt.

But how much distance? Could they even go home? Would they be safe there?

It was the unknown that bothered him. Why did her aunt want to harm Mona? What was her endgame?

And now they were not only cat owners, but they could now call themselves proud wolf owners. A wolf. Was that even legal to own?

"Take a right."

Mason jerked at Mona's sudden demand. "What?"

"Take a right. Right here." She pointed, tapping on the window.

Scatter meowed.

Bozo growled low.

Geez. Okay. They all wanted him to turn right.

He turned right onto a dirt road that looked to be leading them directly into the dark—extremely dark—forest.

Nothing good ever happened in dark, spooky forests.

"Why did we just turn right, Mona? We should be getting the hell out of here." A cold draft touched his arm. He shivered.

"You felt that, didn't you? The coldness?"

"I did."

"I don't know who it is, but I trust them."

"Uh?" Mason gripped the steering wheel harder. The night just kept getting weirder and weirder. "What do you mean?"

"Slow down, Mason." Mona clutched his arm, her fingers like icicles. "Turn off the lights."

He followed her directions. "Mona?"

"Stop the car."

Geez. She needed to start telling him what the hell was going on.

He put the car in park and then grabbed her hand, pulling it up for a kiss. "What is going on?"

"I think there's a ghost in here. They whispered to me in the house. They just whispered for us to turn and to stop here."

"A ghost?"

Although it was hard to make out all her features sitting in the dark—in the very spooky woods—he knew Mona was giving him an exasperated expression.

"Don't you believe in ghosts, Mason?"

Oh, his sweet Mona and her silly jokes.

"So, what does this ghost want us to do?" And why was Mona always able to communicate with ghosts? Like him, at one time.

"To get out of the car."

Scatter meowed quietly.

Bozo whimpered.

Yep, he totally agreed.

He didn't want to get out of the car either.

FOLLOW THAT GHOST

MONA STEPPED out of the car and waited while Scatter and Bozo lumbered out after her, then she shut her door quietly. Barely a click could be heard. Mason must've been watching her intently because he mirrored her actions.

She couldn't say why she thought she had to shut her door quiet as a mouse—because there had been no whispering in her ear to do so—she just did.

"Okay, what now?" Mason whispered as he walked to her side.

Mona glanced at her surroundings, a shiver running down her spine at how dark it was. The trees hovering around them didn't allow for much moonlight to slip through. The car lights were out.

They were essentially plunged into darkness.

"Mona?" Mason grabbed her hand as he whispered her name a bit harshly.

She knew he hadn't meant to. It was his nerves peeking out, and his worry for them. He worried so much all the time, especially about her.

She met his gaze, his eyes glowing brightly in the night.

A blue-greenish tint. How odd. She had never seen his eyes glow in the dark before.

"I have no idea." She shrugged, smiling a bit at Mason's irritated frown. "I heard the whisper that said get out of the car, and now, nothing."

"Seriously?"

A small giggle slipped out at Mason's annoyed tone. She stiffened when Scatter hissed and Bozo growled.

"That can't be good," Mason said in a hushed tone. He stepped in front of her as if shielding her from some unknown enemy.

Bozo started sniffing the ground and moved forward. Scatter followed.

"We should get back in the car."

Mona disagreed. The voice told her to get out of the car. There had to have been a reason.

She started walking in the same direction the animals went, tugging on Mason's hand.

"This is a bad idea, my sweet Mona."

Yeah, it probably was. But she enacted bad ideas all the time. She bought a haunted house and look how that almost turned out.

She also met the love of her life, so it wasn't a completely terrible idea. She could only assume something good would come out of this new adventure.

As they walked farther into the deep, dark forest, she started to worry Mason might be more right than she wanted to admit.

It was still difficult to see. Branches swayed above them, trees outlining their path, barely allowing any moonlight to pass through. They hadn't stopped to grab a flashlight from the trunk. Although her eyes had adjusted somewhat, she still tripped on fallen branches or patches of leaves that fooled you by hiding a tiny hole in the path.

She kept ahold of Mason's hand the entire time. Bozo and Scatter were never too far ahead.

Bozo suddenly stopped. As did Scatter.

Mason squeezed her hand when an eerie bluish glow appeared in front of them. About twenty feet away.

"You see that, right?" he whispered.

"Oh, yeah." The color reminded her of Mason's eyes. She tugged on his hand. "Look at me."

He turned his head, his eyes glowing an iridescent blue. "What's the matter?"

She wasn't sure. So, she didn't answer.

Turning back to the hovering blue mass, she stared, wondering. Could it be?

Then she whipped her gaze back at Mason, who had turned his head to stare at the odd light as well. Gripping his face, comforted by his smooth beard, she whispered, "Look at me."

A low masculine chuckle echoed between them as he turned back in her direction. Her hand on his cheek didn't give him much of a choice. "I just did. What's going on, my sweet Mona?"

She brushed her hand across his forehead and down his beard, staring into his brilliant, beautiful eyes that glimmered in the night. "Your eyes are glowing. Like that light in front of us. I think that's the ghost."

Mason stiffened. "I'm not a ghost anymore. Your eyes are kind of glowing, too."

She tilted her head, giving him an exasperated look he probably couldn't see very well. "Not like yours, I'm sure."

"We can't keep walking blindly in this forest. And we especially can't start following a big blue light that appeared out of nowhere. We need to turn around and get the hell out of here."

Come.

Mona trembled at the soft voice that once again whispered in her ear and darted her gaze to the blue glowing mass. It started to move away from them.

"Follow that ghost." Mona grabbed his hand and tugged. "We can't lose it."

"This is insane," Mason whispered, yet followed her, although she didn't give him much of a choice as her grip was strong and unyielding.

Bozo and Scatter led the way, following the blue orb as it floated ahead of them.

As suddenly as it appeared, it vanished.

They all froze.

Mona pinned her gaze straight ahead, her brows puckering at a new light she could see. A normal light, if she had to guess.

"It looks like a tiny house."

"Yeah, and tiny houses in the middle of dark, scary woods are never *nice* tiny houses."

She chuckled. "Well, we won't know if we don't check it out."

"This is still a bad idea," Mason muttered, but he followed along as they edged closer to the house.

Bozo and Scatter stopped near the tree line as she and Mason crept closer to the window that was lit up with yellow merry light.

Being careful not to make a sound, they both peered through the window. Mona gasped and ducked low. Mason crouched close to her, breathing heavily.

"Okay. I'd say we found the vampires' nest," he whispered. "And we didn't bring the stakes or ax with. We're defenseless."

"But are we?" She grasped his cheek. "The ghost wanted us to come here. It didn't whisper to grab any weapons."

"They're vampires. You saw what I saw. One looked to be drinking blood out of a glass. And the teeth. You had to have seen the teeth on that big dude. He is seriously big."

"Well, drinking out of a glass sounds very refined, not monsterish at all."

Mason groaned. "I have a feeling you're about to do something I won't like."

"Probably."

Mona patted his cheek, then stood up and walked briskly to the front door before he could stop her.

Then she knocked.

THAT WASN'T WHAT I WAS
EXPECTING

MASON SWORE he felt his heart drop right out of his chest when Mona knocked on the door. She was hell on wheels, fast as the devil. She had stood up and walked so swiftly to the door, he didn't even have time to process what she was about to do.

Jerking to his feet, he met her by the door just as it swung open.

Great.

The big dude with the very large teeth stood in front of them.

"I was wondering how long it would take you to knock on the door. You're as pretty as your mother was." The big dude then produced a wide grin, displaying his sharp fangs with clarity.

"Your mother wasn't killed by a vampire, was she?" Mason whispered.

Mona frowned and shook her head. "I'm pretty sure he can hear your whispering, Mason."

The dude's toothy grin expanded even more. "Excellent hearing. It comes with the territory."

Which meant the guy could probably hear his heart was pounding like a pogo stick going haywire. Just great.

Then the guy swept his arm to the side and tilted his head in invitation. "Come on in to our humble abode."

Next, he'd ask them to kindly sit down and display their necks with a cheery smile.

They were about to die.

By nice vampires.

Mona grabbed his hand, squeezing delicately as if she knew his fear was skyrocketing. "Thank you so much. I'm Mona, which you must've guessed since you knew my mother. And this is Mason."

Then she tugged them inside the house. A hard tug, too, because he refused to move his feet at first.

"I'm Joe." The big guy pointed to his friend by the table with the glass of blood still in his hand. He was dressed in a nice, white buttoned shirt with crisp black pants. "That's Donnie."

Mason tried to hide the horror and terrifying fear coursing through his veins when two more guys walked into the room.

They were totally outnumbered.

Joe smiled at his friends and pointed to the fellow on the right dressed in a flannel shirt and dark-blue jeans. "That's Peter." He pointed to the other man dressed in a pair of sweats and a black T-shirt. "That's George."

The big man himself was dressed in khaki pants and a white shirt that filled out his form. It showed every muscle in clear definition. Mason didn't consider himself a weak man, but put up against this guy, he knew he'd lose the fight.

"How'd you know we'd knock?" Mona asked as she nodded at each man with a smile that told Mason she wasn't scared at all.

Well, he was scared enough for both of them.

Donnie took a sip of his drink and grinned, displaying his perfect fangs. "We caught your scent when you got close to the cabin." He set his drink down. "We're glad you came. This makes it easier."

Yeah, to kill them with no witnesses. They were out in the middle of nowhere with no house or human or living creature in sight. Mason figured even the animals in the woods didn't come near this cabin.

"What's that?"

How could Mona sound so calm? And why in the hell wasn't he saying anything? He should be speaking up and protecting her.

"To contact you." Joe's happy, toothy grin faded. "We need your help."

"My help?" Mona sounded confused.

Oh, Mason was beyond confused as well. Why would they help vampires? Not only were they surrounded in a nest of vampires, but they were also crazy out-of-their-mind vampires.

"Joe's right. You look so much like your mother." Donnie's eyes glistened as if he were about to shed a tear. "She was a very kind, wonderful woman. She kept us safe."

"Seriously?"

All eyes turned to him the moment he uttered a word he hadn't meant to slip. But they were supposed to believe that?

Donnie nodded, then focused his attention on Mona. "What did your mother tell you?"

"Nothing. She didn't tell me anything. I found her journal, but it gives me more questions than answers. And my aunt—"

"Ya can't trust her," Peter said, cutting her off, taking a step toward her. "She be da worst kind of witch."

Mona trembled. "Well, we didn't get a good vibe from her."

That was an understatement.

"Do you mean witch, as in literally, a witch?" Mason decided to ask.

Peter nodded, his eyes round with terror. "Da worst kind."

Donnie stepped closer, his expression soft, his stance nonthreatening. Out of all four vampires, he appeared to hold the air of authority. With his impeccable clothes, his hair combed back with debonair grace, and the way all three men always looked to him for guidance, Mason assumed he was their leader.

"What does your mother's journal say? Anything about us?"

Mona squeezed his hand. "Well, not you specifically. No names. Just details about vampires. Heightened sense of smell. Strong. Night vision. Drinks blood. Things like that."

Donnie nodded. "And did it say how to kill a vampire?"

"Well..." Mona hesitated and looked at him. He didn't know what to say. He had yet to read her mother's journal, as Mona never offered to let him and he didn't think it was his place to ask. "No, it didn't. I'll be honest, we came to help my aunt with a vampire problem, and I brought with supplies I thought would work based on what I saw online."

"Your mother was a good woman. Kind and thoughtful. She was also a witch. Think more Glinda than the Wicked Witch of the West," Donnie said. "She protected us. Protected all kinds of creatures. If you look through her journal, you'll probably find she never once wrote down how to kill them."

Mona turned and placed her hand on his chest, gasping. "The ghost. Maybe that's my mother. Maybe she led us here to protect these men from my aunt. We have to help them. He's right. She never mentions how to kill any creature in her journal."

Oh, his sweet Mona.

Taking the word of a vampire.

But since he loved her and trusted her with all his heart, he was going to have faith that she knew what she was doing.

"Okay."

The bright smile that lit up her face started to calm the racing of his heart.

Then he looked at Donnie. "But don't think I won't protect Mona with everything I have if you do something that I don't like."

"We protected Mona's mother as best as we could. And we'll protect Mona as well. Marcella is strong, though. She's only getting stronger." Donnie gave a halfhearted chuckle. "And I'm sorry, Mona, but the ghost in the woods isn't your mother. That's Cory. He's been roaming this area for as long as we've lived here. He only appears when he wants to."

Mason felt her excitement disappear like a balloon popping without notice as Mona's shoulders sagged by the news.

"We can't stay here. We sort of ran from my aunt and..." Mona shrugged as she laughed a little. "She wasn't too happy. She obviously doesn't think she can kill all four of you by herself, which is why she called me. But we can't take the chance. We should go."

Donnie's expression fell into sorrow, his eyes sparkling with concern. "I don't think she called you to ask for help. As much as I hate to admit it, that woman probably could kill all four of us. Not that we wouldn't fight hard. I would say she's finally making her move."

Oh, Mason didn't like the sound of that.

"What move?"

Donnie met his gaze. In that moment, Mason knew he could trust this vampire with his life. The look in his eyes. So raw and real and full of compassion.

"She wants Mona's powers. She has to kill her to gain them." Donnie paused. "Why do you think she's so powerful now? She killed…"

"My mother," Mona finished on a whisper. She shook her head as the grip on his hand tightened. "That wasn't what I was expecting. How could she? I wasn't there when my mother died. It was a car crash. I don't understand."

Mason lifted her hand and kissed the back of it, then cupped her chin so she would look at him. "That's probably why she never mentioned your aunt. She wanted to protect you."

"Then she should've armed me with every possible knowledge I should know. I don't even know how to be a witch. Like, what do I do? How do I protect these men?"

Mason smiled and kissed her softly. "The same thing you did for me. You just do it. It'll come naturally."

Oh, and he had no doubt they'd conquer this problem, too.

Mona was a force to be reckoned with.

THAT WAS WEIRD

MONA INHALED AND EXHALED, her hands crunching together in tight fists, then relaxing. Her eyes opened and closed with excruciating gentleness.

No matter what she did, the picture before her didn't change.

"We don't have to do this," Mason whispered, then grabbed her hands before she could do another round of squeezing them together into a tight vice.

Well, he was right. They didn't have to.

They *needed* to.

And the dilapidated house stood before her like it was swept out of a scary movie and plopped down with a big whoosh would be their salvation.

Which was odd, because a month ago it had been their nightmare.

She tightened her grip with Mason's hand and smiled at him. "We got this. And where else are we going to hide four vampires from an evil witch?"

He tilted his head with an odd expression as if he were

truly contemplating the question. The very silly, outrageous question no one should ever have to ask.

"Good point. I doubt your aunt will think to look for us here, and by the time she does, we'll be prepared." He scrunched his brows together. "Right?"

"Totally prepared."

"Ya sure this be da best place for us?" Pete asked as he approached the house to Mona's left.

"Absolutely sure," she replied with as much confidence as she could.

She was *so* not sure at all. For all she knew, the moment they stepped through the threshold, the evil being—or whatever they fought—would jump out and swallow them whole.

"It's very..." Donnie cleared his throat. "Pleasant. I'm sure it's lovely inside."

Mona peered around Mason to smile at Donnie. How kind of him to pretend. And he really was a nice man—vampire—vampire man.

After they dropped the bomb at her feet that her mother had been murdered by her aunt, who now wanted to kill her, they left. As fast as their feet would carry them. Her car had been in the same spot as they left it, nothing sinister seemed to have happened to it. No weird spell or whatever. Not that she would know if a spell had been cast on her car. But she sensed it was safe.

But she hadn't thought it silly to wonder whether a spell or hex of some sort had been cast on her vehicle because how else had her aunt killed her mother. She really wanted to know.

The four vampires followed in a vehicle of their own.

Mason argued with her the entire way when she had

told everyone where they could lay low until they had a solid plan of attack.

The creepy old house she purchased for a steal.

"So." Donnie cleared his throat again. "Shall we venture inside?"

Yes, they should. If her feet could find it in themselves to move.

"Mona..." Mason whispered. "My sweet Mona. We really don't have to do this."

She exhaled, then let go of Mason's hand before he could try to discourage her one more time. They had to do this. It was the only safe place for all eight of them. Two humans, one previously a ghost, four vampires, one black cat, and one wolf.

Since she was the owner of this despicable house, she had to step inside first.

She unlocked the door with shaky hands, but quickly, just in case Mason tried to stop her, and swung open the door. Before she could chicken out, she walked inside and flicked on the lights.

Everyone else followed behind her. She didn't see Mason until he grabbed her hand. His touch felt icy cold.

That was weird.

Oh no.

Was that why he was so adamant they shouldn't come back here? Was that why he seemed so apprehensive to stay away?

Because if he walked back inside, he would turn into a ghost once again.

She jerked her head at Donnie, the fright no doubt evident in her eyes. "Can you see Mason?"

Donnie arched a brow and nodded. "I can."

She shoved her hand out of his and stared hard at

Donnie, considering when she first met Mason she could never see him unless they were touching. "Can you still see him?"

This time both of Donnie's brows lifted. "I can still see him. He's looking very relieved. Something we should know?"

A low chuckle drifted to her ear as a warm hand grasped hers. She turned toward Mason, who had a very, very relieved smile on his face.

So maybe the coldness was coming from her hand because nothing but warmth seeped from his.

"You were worried, admit it," she commanded.

Mason nodded. "Obviously for nothing. All is well."

She slapped his shoulder. Not hard, but enough to wipe the smile from his face. "Next time tell me why you don't want to do something. If you would've...if you had changed...if you—"

A sweet kiss touched her lips, cutting off her stammering. The warmth from his mouth and the tenderness from his kiss helped to settle her nerves.

"I'm sorry, my sweet Mona. Forgive me. I'll say something next time."

She rested her forehead against his. "You better."

"I say, the inside of this house looks much better than the outside," Joe said as he looked around the large foyer, his gaze darting up the wide staircase.

"Yes, don't let the appearance fool you. It once held the wonders of evil," Mona said with a laugh. She spread her arms wide. "Welcome to my home that I haven't even slept in for one night. Where Mason lived for fifty years as a ghost before I came along. Countless women murdered and their souls trapped in dolls. And who knows if the evil is even gone. Take your pick where you'd like to sleep."

All four vampires stared at her wide-eyed. Then Donnie smoothed his worried expression into a gentle smile. "I'm sure a few spells to ward off the evil will do the trick. Thank you for inviting us here. We're very appreciative."

Mona looked at Donnie wide-eyed this time. "But I don't know any spells. That's the problem. I don't have any clue how to keep you safe."

Donnie's smile didn't waver. "You are Mona Cordero. You are the daughter of the kindest witch I have ever known. You are a powerful witch. And I have every faith in you." Then his smile inched up even higher. "And your mother left you her journal. I think if you look hard, you might find the answers you're seeking."

Mona's purse—more like a fanciful satchel— hung across her body, the weight of it calling to her. Because inside lay her journal. She always carried it with her since finding it. It made her feel closer to her mother.

Perhaps Donnie was right.

Maybe all she needed to do was look a little harder and the answers would reveal themselves.

A CLOSE CALL

MASON LEANED AGAINST THE COUNTER, petting Scatter, who had jumped up next to him.

"Yeah, you're right, Scatter. That was...a close call."

Meow.

"I know. I know. I should've mentioned my apprehensions to Mona. But then she wouldn't have come here, and as crazy as it might seem, this is the safest place for her. I only want her to be safe."

Meoooow.

Mason bent, getting face-to-face with Scatter as he rubbed gingerly under his neck, Scatter's favorite place to be petted. "I promise to be open and honest with her about everything from here on out. You have my word. Enough with the third-degree."

Scatter whipped his tail back and forth and purred.

Then a soft growl echoed near him. Mason looked down at the floor where Bozo sat, baring his teeth. Just a fraction. To get his point across.

Mason rolled his eyes. "Wow. You're laying into me, too. You barely know Mona."

Bozo stood up and growled again.

"Oh, you know all you need to know. Well, I've known her longer. I didn't want to worry her. You two have nothing to worry about. I swear I won't keep anything from her again."

A menacing growl and a sharp meow answered him at the exact same time. Scatter and Bozo weren't messing around. They were ganging up on him.

At one point in his life, he would've never imagined he could speak to animals. And he wouldn't say he could actually hear words coming out of their mouths. He just instinctively knew what they were saying, responding in kind.

Mona didn't seem to think it was odd. Nor did the vampires.

Reaching down, he petted Bozo, scratching under his neck as he had with Scatter. Bozo responded by nudging his hand with his nose to keep doing it.

"I'm glad you're on our side, Bozo. Welcome to the... family."

Scatter jumped down from the counter and started to walk away. Bozo followed. Obviously, the conversation was over. Then they both strolled out of the kitchen as if they owned the house.

Silence enveloped the room. A comfortable silence.

Although he had dreaded coming back to this house, he didn't feel a malevolent spirit. It just felt...secure.

Mason felt her presence before he heard her. Turning around, he smiled before opening his arms, indicating he wanted her to come closer.

She complied, resting her body against his.

"What's the matter, my sweet Mona? It's been a long day. We should go to sleep. The other guys have." He assumed Scatter and Bozo were about to find a place to sleep as well.

She shivered. Thankfully, not because he was a cold, chilly ghost once again. It had been a real concern for him the entire drive.

"Mona?"

She lifted her head, then backed away and laid her journal on the counter. "I'm not tired. I don't think I could sleep if I tried. I've been reading my mom's journal again."

He knew she was determined to find a way to protect everyone. While she curled up on the couch in the living room, he had stocked the shelves with the food they purchased on the way and found a room for their stuff. He decided to pick the one closest to the stairs, and as far away from the room where the dolls had been. He never wanted to step foot in that room again. Donnie, the leader of the vampires, had chosen that room.

"You also can't wear yourself out. You need to rest."

She tapped her journal. "I need ingredients. For a spell."

His brow rose. "I thought there were no spells in the book."

"I had to look really hard. I had to read between the lines. Here, look." Mona started to flip through the pages until she found the one she wanted.

April 11, 1993

Today was a beautiful day. Mona loves being outside and smelling the flowers, the white heather and gladiolus flowers the most. She always gets dirty playing in the sand. But thankfully, she enjoys the water, so bath time is never a trial. I'm blessed she's such a joyful child. She loves singing in the bath. One of her favorite tunes that she insists I sing first every time. Mix it all together, and you have a very strong home. That's all I ever want.

Mason read the short passage. "You do enjoy singing in the shower."

Mona nudged his shoulder as she chuckled. "You're missing the point. The answers are all right there. The white heather flower symbolizes protection. The gladiolus symbolizes strength. Mix those with a bit of sand and water, bless them, and I have my ingredients."

He re-read the passage again, noting how a few words were slightly bolder than the rest, sticking out. He probably would've never noticed it if she hadn't pointed it out.

"And the spell?"

"She always sang one particular song to me during bath time." Mona's smile widened. "My mother was teaching me all along, and I didn't know it. She sang to me all the time, different songs. I think each song is a different spell. I know exactly what spell to use to protect this house. We need to get the rest of the ingredients."

WHAT'S UP WITH THAT?

MONA WIPED her brow with the back of her hand, wiggled her nose to make the itch go away, then went right back to stirring.

The kitchen was a disaster.

Pots, pans, bowls, spoons, and ingredients galore littered every available counterspace.

Okay, so she wasn't exactly the tidiest baker. Not that she was baking, per se. Concocting different potions didn't fall under the baking category. But that's what her kitchen looked like at the moment. Like a baking disaster had exploded.

After she had deciphered a few passages in her journal and wrote down everything she needed, she sent Mason and Donnie on a supply run. She could tell Mason hadn't wanted to leave her alone, but after a few short words with Scatter and Bozo, he relented.

Neither animal had left her side as she continued to decode her journal in the living room on the most comfortable couch she had ever sat on. Honestly, she couldn't understand how the outside of the house looked like it leapt right out of a horror movie and the inside looked like it should be featured in a glamorous magazine.

By the time Mason and Donnie returned, unfortunately, the next morning as some of the things she had needed weren't available in the area, she was ninety-five percent confident—well, okay, eighty-five percent confident—the spell would work.

While she knew Mason and Donnie didn't get any sleep, neither had she. She didn't leave the spot from the couch for much. Her hand had even started to cramp from all the writing, but she didn't stop. She wanted to jot down every song she remembered. She knew every entry her mother wrote—and it was a thick journal—had a spell hidden in there. That was a lot of songs. She was afraid she wouldn't be able to remember every song that her mother ever sang.

But she refused to give up.

As soon as Mason and Donnie had dropped off all her supplies in the kitchen, Donnie left to get some rest. They had made it back before the sun rose. While he had been gone, his friends had covered every window in their bedrooms to keep them safe from the sunlight until night reappeared.

Mason had insisted she rest as well, but she couldn't. She had to mix up the ingredients for the protection spell. The priority was to protect them, then she could rest. Mason being stubborn, stayed with her.

It took her a while to find the ingredients she needed, and by the time she had it all prepared, the sun had appeared with a welcoming smile.

And that was when her confidence level dipped. She had the potion. She knew the spell. But what did she do with the potion?

Sprinkle it everywhere?

Pour it around the border of the entire house? Which meant she didn't have enough potion.

In the end, she decided to douse the front door as she said the spell—in a sort of sing-song voice. She couldn't help it as that was how she had been taught the words. Her mother always sang it. She figured the front door was her best bet because if you wanted to enter, you had to come through the front door. It symbolized the threshold of the house.

Shivers had run up and down her spine when she sang the last word. A small burst of air had brushed against her skin.

It hadn't been frightening. But it had been a sign. She had secured the house.

Shortly after, she sent Mason, who hadn't left her side once, to bed. He could barely keep his eyes open. While she should've gotten some sleep herself, she had more potions to prepare. They had a witch to vanquish—her aunt.

Thinking about it made her ill, so she tried not to think about it. Instead, she worked.

Which was why the kitchen was a mess.

A low growl by her feet had her pausing as she was about to drop some rose oil into her latest potion.

She glanced at Bozo sitting by her, surprised to see the hair standing up on his back and his sharp fangs ready to pounce.

"Bozo?"

Flinching, she watched as Scatter jumped off the counter and raced out of the kitchen. Bozo didn't move a muscle, although his growls became louder.

"Mason?"

Where was he? With a glance at the clock on the wall, she realized more time had passed than she thought. It was two o'clock in the afternoon. Perhaps she should check on him.

And find out why Scatter and Bozo were suddenly on edge. It couldn't be their vampire friends because it was still daylight out. They wouldn't risk leaving their bedrooms when the other rooms in the house weren't completely covered with curtains.

Grabbing a few bottles of potions she had already made, stuffing them in her pocket, she left the kitchen. The small front room—the room she loved to call her parlor— furnished with a bookshelf and a tiny cozy chair was empty, as was the foyer. Nothing seemed amiss.

A loud screeching sound pierced the walls. As if Scatter had cried out in pain.

"What's up with that? Scatter never gets hurt," Mona whispered to Bozo, who snapped and growled like he was fighting an invincible enemy. She looked at him, shocked.

What was going on?

But thankfully, Bozo didn't run off as Scatter had.

Gazing up the long staircase, goose bumps flushed her skin.

Bozo growled again.

Making eye contact with him, she nodded, then started climbing. They needed to find out what happened to Scatter and check on everyone else. Something was clearly wrong.

Her heart started to hammer with each step. Louder and louder. Each foot forward felt like she was taking her last step, as if her world was about to end.

Something evil—malevolent—waited for her at the top.

Oh, no.

This had been a terrible idea to come back.

This house wasn't safe.

It was the epitome of evil.

They had never truly confirmed whether they destroyed the evil being or not.

Obviously not.

When she hit the top step, a loud roaring sound echoed in her ears. Then her eyes glided to the door Mason had picked for their bedroom.

Her hand shook as she glided toward it. Then, right before she twisted it open, her other hand dove in her pocket and clutched the potion bottles cuddled together.

The door creaked open.

Mason sat in the middle of the room on a chair, his body slumped over. He looked dead, his eyes closed, his skin pale, white as a ghost. She was afraid if she touched him to confirm it, he'd feel cold to the touch.

She should've never stayed huddled in the kitchen, working herself to the bone. Because now she'd lose Mason to the nefarious villain standing behind him.

Her hands clutched the bottles tighter.

Or not.

FROM OUT OF NOWHERE

"Ah, you decided to join us, Mona? Please come in," her aunt said with a cackle and a vile smirk. She waved a hand for Mona to come farther into the room.

Mona took a few steps, but only to get a better look at her surroundings, not because she told her to do so. The bed looked as if Mason had been sleeping and was ripped out from under the covers, which lay tangled half on the bed, half on the floor.

Scatter was sprawled near the end of the bed, still as could be. She couldn't detect whether he was breathing or not. Nor could she about Mason.

At least she had Bozo by her side. With the sun shining brightly through the window, she knew their new vampire friends would not be any help.

"What did you do to Mason?" She tried to ask in a confident voice, but she was afraid it came out more timid than she wanted.

Marcella shrugged. "You seem to be the expert. You tell me." An evil laugh escaped. "The protection spell was nicely done. It's too bad I was already inside the house, otherwise, it would've worked."

Well, that was disheartening to learn. If only she would've been a little faster at creating it. Her aunt had been in the house for quite a while because she had been in the kitchen creating more potions for at least a few hours. Why had she waited so long to make an appearance?

But thank goodness she had.

Her hand clutched the three bottles she had snatched from the counter. When should she use them?

Better question, would she remember the spell correctly? Because she knew exactly what spell to use.

"Only one thing is going to happen here. You will relinquish your powers," Marcella winced mockingly, "which, unfortunately, means you have to die. And once you do, I'll let your sweet boyfriend live." She raised her hand, her thumb and middle finger pressed together. "Or I can snap my fingers and he dies right now."

Both choices were terrible. Of course, Mona was never one to do well when given an ultimatum. Nobody told her what to do.

But she also didn't want Mason to die. He didn't deserve any of this.

Bozo growled low, still standing strong by her side.

Hmm. So Bozo didn't like ultimatums either.

They stared at each other for the longest time. Neither said a word. Not even Bozo, although she could feel the tension emanating from him.

"My mother never told me about you. She didn't tell me that I was a...witch." Mona's eyes narrowed. "But she raised me exactly the way she meant to. She gave me everything I needed without saying a word about her secret. I can feel the energy flowing through my veins. I can feel her spirit and guidance. Those two options suck. Try again."

As strange as it was, as soon as she said every word, she felt it. Her mother's presence. Calm swept through her, just like all the times when she fell ill and her mother made everything better.

She could do this.

She didn't want to hurt her aunt, but it had to be done.

"You're an insolent child. You are no match to me."

Mona smiled. "And my mother obviously frightened you —that you were no match for her—that you had to kill her."

Without hesitating, Mona dug her hand out of her pocket and threw all three vials at Marcella's feet. Each bottle shattered, the contents slipping into the floorboards and onto Marcella's shoes.

"As long as night is night and day is day, you will stay without the right and without delay.

Be gone you, be gone away. It's forever true, and come what may."

From out of nowhere, a jewelry box fell at Marcella's feet, the lid popping open. Mona watched in equal horror and fascination as her aunt vanished before her eyes and the lid to the box snapped shut.

Bozo slapped a paw on top of the box.

She hadn't even felt him leave her side, but apparently, he had. He knocked the box to the ground and helped her.

She couldn't believe it worked, and so well.

Of course, it helped she used all three potions together. One potion to immobilize her. One potion to make her lose her ability to speak. One potion to bind her for eternity.

One spell, when said with all three potions, worked like a charm—apparently. She honestly hadn't been sure it would work when she made each potion.

Her mother used to sing that particular song when she had nightmares. She always told her it would vanquish the monsters and they'd never return. Mona hoped that was true.

Rushing to the box, she patted Bozo on the head, smiled, and picked up the box. "Good boy. You were amazing. Go downstairs and grab another protection spell for me. We need to make sure she can't escape and no one can open this box."

Bozo licked her on the face and then ran out of the room.

She scooted closer to Mason, almost afraid to touch him.

Then her warm hand touched his cold skin.

"I love you, Mason. You can't leave me."

Wrapping her hand within his, she closed her eyes and said a silent prayer. Then she focused on all the energy coursing through her veins, willing it to flow straight to his.

Her fingers tingled, then a sharp zing zapped her entire body.

Mason inhaled and sat up. He blinked a few times, his eyes struggling to remain open. But what comforted her most was the warmth that radiated from his hand.

She had no idea what she did—or how she even did it—but she was grateful. Losing Mason would be like losing herself. She knew it with certainty.

"What happened? What did I miss?" he asked in a whisper as he pulled her closer and kissed her softly on the lips.

"Not much. My aunt put some sort of spell on you. Threatened to kill you and take my powers. Then I defeated her by putting her in this tiny box and somehow saved you with a power I really need to get a handle on."

Mason glanced at the box in her hand, then at her hand

still securely in his. "Oh, that's it?" He chuckled. "I didn't doubt you for a second. We'll figure your powers out together. You and me. The evilinators."

Mona giggled. "We definitely will, but we'll have to think of a new name. I think I'm meant to help different beings and creatures, not kill them. I'm a good witch."

Bozo took that moment to stop by her side and dropped the potion.

"First things first." Begrudgingly, she let go of his hand and grabbed the potion. She dumped the entire contents all over the box while singing the spell. They were safe from her aunt. Elation and so much relief hit her.

Then she bundled Scatter in her arms and did the same thing she had for Mason. A few seconds later, Scatter opened his eyes, meowed, then jumped out of her arms.

"You're welcome." Mona shook her head as Scatter walked out of the room, Bozo following closely behind him.

Mason eyed the box. "So, what do we do with that?"

Mona didn't even glance at it. "Well, we have a perfectly scary basement to keep it in." She laughed as Mason groaned.

Then he wrapped his arms around her and pulled her in for a kiss.

Soft and languid, yet full of passion.

With Mason by her side—or in her arms—they could conquer anything.

THE START OF A NEW PATH

MONA GLANCED up as Joe walked into the kitchen, smiled, then went back to stirring her latest potion.

"Mason finished mowing the lawn. Sure wish we could've helped. It looked like hard work," Joe said as he leaned against the counter and watched her.

She imagined it *was* hard work. The grass had to be at least a foot tall, if not more. Unfortunately, Mason had to do it by himself since their vampire friends couldn't venture outside during the day. It would look odd if they mowed at night.

Although, she was very proud of herself. After much digging and deciphering, she found a spell in her mother's journal that cloaked the windows and protected the vampires during the daylight. Now they could walk around the house without fear. Of course, to anyone who happened to look at the house from the outside, everything would look normal.

Within the last week, she had seen those mischievous boys walking past her house. As long as the neighborhood boys kept their distance and didn't cause her problems, she wouldn't get all spooky on them. She was a bit tempted to embellish the story they knew about Old Man Bennett. Of course, it was only a story. She had yet to feel a ghostly presence from this so-called Old Man Bennett they talked about.

But she was ready if he ever appeared. To either help him cross over to the light...or vanquish him to the netherworlds.

After a week of studying, she had tons of potions ready and waiting. She wanted to be prepared for anything. By all the accounts from Donnie and the other three vampires, there were too many evil beings out there. Not all creatures were friendly.

So she prepared.

Potion after potion.

The kitchen was a disaster. Still.

Despite her aunt locked in a box, tucked securely away in the doom-and-gloom basement—which she cast a strong spell on to contain the evil—their vampire friends decided to stick around. They had much to tell her.

Stories about her mother.

Stories about other creatures.

Stories to arm her with the knowledge she needed to defeat any villain that crossed her path.

"You've been a great help. I appreciate everything you've done," Mona finally replied as she added another ingredient to her latest potion.

And she was grateful to their new friends. She had wanted a shelf for her potions in the kitchen, so they built one for her. They had also done some cleaning and other odds and ends that she asked of them.

All in all, it had been a very productive week.

She and Mason were finally gaining a better perspective of their lives and where to go from here.

Donnie also had connections. A few days ago, documents arrived in the mail. Mason officially had paperwork showing he was, in fact, not dead. As much as she wanted him by her side all the time, he needed something for himself. Tomorrow, he intended on applying for the position of a detective. And it made sense. They needed money. She currently didn't have a job.

While she might be learning a lot about her mother and who she really was, they needed money to sustain themselves.

She had no doubt Mason would get the job. He was smart and intuitive and very, very determined.

"Need any other help?" Joe asked. "We finished adding that bookshelf you wanted in your bedroom."

Mona smiled. "Thank you. I'm good for now. You probably need to rest."

Although she had protected the windows, they normally slept during the day.

Joe nodded and left her to finish her task.

Bozo and Scatter kept her company. They enjoyed resting on their soft, comfy beds they bought for them. She had arranged it in the corner of the kitchen where they had an excellent view of the entire room. They wanted to be prepared for anything as well. She couldn't have asked for better protectors. Bozo was in a good sleep. His tiny snores made her grin every so often.

She inhaled and sighed happily when a warm pair of arms circled her waist and then a tender kiss hit her neck.

"Aww, my sweet Mona, you're working too much," Mason said in a low timbre as his lips trailed a path across her neck and to her ear.

And *he* smelled delicious. Clean and fresh with a hint of cinnamon spice.

"So are you. I hear the lawn is finished. You obviously just took your—what—third shower of the day." Low laughter escaped as he nuzzled her neck.

"Only my second one, thank you very much. We're hiring a lawn company from here on out. That was brutal."

Mona chuckled. No doubt, he wasn't exaggerating.

"Let's take a break. Both of us."

She really wanted to. Then her eyes hit all of the ingredients scattered across the kitchen counter. But she also wanted to keep working.

Before she could answer, Mason swung her around and kissed her sweetly on the lips, leaning into her. All his delicious parts molded into hers. As if they were made for each other. The kiss was slow and delicate, yet filled with such emotion. He was always so gentle with her.

"You need a break." He grinned wickedly before snatching another kiss. "Let me hold you. Let me love you. Let me show you how special you are."

Oh, this man. His endearing words and exquisite touch. It always did things to her she never imagined was possible.

How could she say no to that?

She couldn't.

"Okay, a tiny break."

The devilish glimmer in his eyes said his version of tiny would be much different from hers.

Then he swooped her into his arms and started walking out of the kitchen, but not before Scatter and Bozo perked their heads up. "Man the fort, boys. And don't come knocking on the door."

Mona giggled. But it was true. Finding time alone, especially with a house full of guests, was not as easy as it was a week ago when it was just the two of them.

But she wouldn't change it for the world.

Soon, she'd do her part to make the world a better place. Keep everyone safe. Humans and creatures alike.

———

A SIMPLE HALLOWEEN

A MONA & MASON MYSTERY - #3

HAPPY HALLOWEEN!

I hope you enjoy the third adventure involving Mona and Mason. This is the first year where I wrote it without using flash fiction prompts. But I thought I'd still use fun chapter titles instead of just numbering them. I hope you enjoy their story...and have a spooktacular holiday...even if you're reading this and it's not actually halloween. Lol

💜 MUCH LOVE,
AMANDA SIEGRIST

SHITS AND GIGGLES

"Do I even want to know what you're doing?"

Mona looked up from the counter, her hands pausing at tying a small burlap bag closed with an orange ribbon dotted with little black witch hats.

"Making fun Halloween bags for the kids."

Mason's brow rose. "We have a huge bowl of candy out in the foyer—if we can even call it a *bowl*. I think having Joe make a coffin to hold the candy was going a little overboard."

He could never resist Mona, especially when she smiled a bright, wicked smile that he knew was the start of trouble.

"Isn't it fun? And he plans to dress up as a vampire."

"He is a vampire."

Mona paused again with the bow. "Well, yeah, but the kids don't know that. He's going for the Dracula look. A little blood hanging down the chin. It's going to be so much fun."

He'd take Mona's word for it. This would be his first Halloween since—well, since turning from a ghost back to human. Five months later, and he was still trying to feel normal again. He barely remembered his childhood. Not that it wasn't a good childhood—he thought so anyway—but even his life right before he died was hard to remember at times. He didn't get the feeling Halloween was a big deal to him over fifty years ago.

With actual vampires in residence, the fact he was a former ghost, and Mona being a witch, drawing attention to their humble home wasn't the best idea. But when Mona wanted something, she always got it.

With Halloween tomorrow night, they didn't have much time to get ready.

He wasn't an expert in anything Mona worked on. Although, he tried to pay attention and ask questions when she worked on a new potion and spell because he knew she liked it. She appreciated he took the time to care about what she was doing. And based on some of the comments from guys at work, they could take a pointer or two from him—not that he'd actually voice it. He'd only been at the precinct as a detective for the last three months and he didn't want to do anything to raise brows. Though, he had faith in Donnie that the paperwork he provided to make him a legit living human being wouldn't fall through. So, his job should be safe. But still. He didn't like to draw too much attention to himself.

Stepping a little closer, his detective skills started to kick him. His eyes zeroed in on the contents sitting on the table. Then to the wicked smile still plastered on his sweet Mona's face.

"Why do I get the feeling these bags are not for every kid?"

"Because they're not." Which she said a little too sweet to his liking.

"What exactly are you putting in those bags? Because I don't see any candy on the counter."

Mona put the bag now tied with the fun Halloween bow to the small pile already formed.

"Oh, there's not candy inside the bag."

Mason tried to keep his patience, especially when dealing with Mona and her *moments*. Over the past five months, since banishing her aunt into a tiny box, putting her in the magically protected basement to live forever, Mona had had more than a few moments. Doing odd things. Saying odd things—more so than usual. Sometimes, even just staring into space. It scared him at times. As if he were slowly losing the woman he loved, and he had no idea why.

"Who are the bags for again?"

Mona's brow rose. "The kids."

Mason countered her sardonic look with a smile. "Which kids?"

"Those little bastards, okay." Then she twisted around and started to pick up the mess she had created.

Three little bags sat on the counter amongst the mess.

Mason didn't even have to ask who *those little bastards* were. He knew. The three neighborhood kids who gave Mona problems all the time. The same kids that were joking around the front yard when she moved in, claiming the house was haunted. For some reason—because he hadn't seen Mona do anything—the kids still thought the house was haunted and that Mona was a witch. Which was funny because it was true.

He wasn't certain, but he figured the three boys wrote on the sidewalk about two weeks ago with chalk. A saying that bothered Mona. 'Witch, witch, go away, never come back another day.' He'd give them points for creativity for trying to match the rain song—not that he'd ever voice it to Mona.

He might've mentioned it to Scatter, who he knew wouldn't tell a soul.

It had rained a week straight. Heavy buckets of rain. Mona had gone outside a few times to collect some of the fresh raindrops. She got soaked to the bone, but she swore it would be useful for some potions. Mason could only assume the boys thought she had conjured the rain, making it stay for as long as it had.

Although they gave her a hard time, the chalk incident not being the only time they treated her like an outcast, it didn't mean Mona should retaliate.

"What's in the bags, my sweet Mona?" he asked softly as he walked up behind her, wrapping his arms around her.

"Nothing much."

He pressed a kiss to her neck, inhaling the subtle scent of ginger. He only recognized the scent because Mona used it a lot in her potions and in a few meals she cooked.

"Mona..."

"It's just a harmless potion. Nothing to worry about."

Yeah, right. Like that was going to convince him to drop the subject.

"Mona..."

She huffed, yet relaxed into his embrace as he peppered a few more kisses along her neck.

"A little bit of this, a little bit of that. Some ginger to ease the pain, and some pepper to enrich the flame. Tease me, taunt me, and I'll show you who gets the last laugh...with a bit of shits and giggles." Then she tapped the bags with a flare of her hand.

Mason couldn't help himself. He laughed, pressing his mouth into her shoulder to hide the sound, even though he knew she heard.

"Oh, my God. You made a spell to give them diarrhea?"

"If they're going to act like little shits, then..." she trailed off as she shrugged.

"And you think they're just going to stand there while you recite that and hand them the bags. I don't think so."

Mona twisted around in his arms, planting a delicious kiss on his lips, the entire time a beautiful, devilish smile splayed across her face.

"Oh, I don't need to say it to them. I just did it. Don't touch those bags unless..." She winked and kissed him again. "Well, unless you want to be glued to the toilet for the night. I'll start supper as soon as I finish cleaning up this mess. So, skedaddle."

Wow.

His sweet Mona sure played him. There was no way in hell he was about to touch any of those bags. Nope. Those little bastards were on their own.

As he walked out of the kitchen, he wondered if the potion would work on everyone, including vampires. Did they even go to the bathroom? He'd seen Donnie, Joe, Peter, and George use the bathroom. Usually to take a shower, but he wasn't sure if they ever used the bathroom for other bodily functions.

He saw Peter lounging in a chair in the parlor reading a book. If he wasn't mistaken, based on the glance to the spine, a book about fairy gardens. He wasn't even going to ask. Peter was an odd guy at times.

His steps slowed to ask Peter about the bathroom and whether he'd be willing to snag the bags from Mona, but then he changed his mind. Maybe the boys needed to learn a lesson.

Don't mess with his Mona.

With the next two days off from work—because Mona wanted him home for Halloween—he wasn't quite sure what to do with himself. Lately, while she worked on her spells and potions, learning everything she could about her mother and the life she missed out on, he worked.

He loved his job. He loved being a detective. Being back in the game felt good. Solving crimes, helping people, being out in the world making a difference. One case at a time.

At least, he tried.

Being new to the department—and partnered with a guy older than him who thought he knew it all—made things difficult at times. But it didn't deter Mason. He knew what the hell he was doing.

Even if he did die from it.

Meow.

Mason stopped in front of the stairs and stared at Scatter. Bozo sat next to him, although didn't make a sound. Usually, they both had something to say when they were together.

"I am not touching those bags, Scatter. You drag them away with your little paws. I'd like to see you sitting in the litter box all night."

Meow.

Mason turned around toward the door at the same time someone knocked.

He knew even before he turned the knob this wouldn't be a pleasant visit.

Tommy, the oldest boy of the trio, stood on the porch with a mixture of terror and anger on his face.

"Is she...is she home?"

The terror seemed to be winning over his anger.

Considering three terrible bags were sitting on the counter, one meant for this little shit, Mason decided getting Mona wouldn't be the best call.

Unless he wasn't asking for Mona, but hoping she wasn't

home. Probably the latter. The bags on the counter said enough.

"What's up?"

"My cat—" Tommy jumped back when Scatter joined him by the doorway, Bozo right behind him. "Oh, you have a cat." Tommy blinked. "And a wolf?"

"Yeah, we do. What about your cat?"

Tommy tore his gaze away from Scatter and Bozo and looked ready to cry. "My cat's missing."

"Well, you came to the right place. I just happen to be a detective."

"I know. I was hoping...You'll help me?"

Meow.

Growl.

Mason smiled at Scatter and Bozo's response, then looked at Tommy. "We sure will."

Thank God, for once their case was simple. No devil in the basement to deal with. No evil witch trying to kill them.

A simple missing cat.

How hard could it be?

SHE'S...A WITCH!

"Ya might wanna come check this out, me Mona."

Mona looked up from the counter, wiping up the last remnants of the mess she had created when making her lovely Halloween bags.

Oh, she wasn't dumb. She saw the disapproval on Mason's face, even in his tone of voice. But enough was enough.

Those annoying neighborhood kids needed to know who they were messing with, and that it wasn't nice to make her life a living hell.

Well, maybe that was exaggerating a bit. But writing cruel words in front of her house, letting their dog poop in her yard, throwing eggs at her front door—oh, yeah, she knew it was them—was enough. She wasn't going to put up with it anymore.

They'd never find out it was her, and that was okay in her book. She only knew it'd make her feel deliriously happy she got them back. This would almost match smashing her beautiful carved pumpkins to smithereens. That hurt the worst. Because she had taken half the day to create those masterpieces, only to have it ruined within an hour.

Just. Cruel.

She had no doubt it was them because she heard their laughter trailing away as they ran down the street right before she peeked outside.

Peter waved a hand in her face when she didn't immediately respond, which was so unusual for her. She always had something to say. It just showed how much those nasty neighborhood boys had been affecting her lately. All she wanted to do was learn everything she could about her powers, and she couldn't. Not when her mind was preoccupied with this nonsense.

"What's the matter?"

By the slight concern in his eyes, something she should've noticed right away, her mind started to race—but for different reasons. What potion did she need to grab? What problems were they about to deal with?

Although they hadn't dealt with anything monumental since her aunt tried to kill them, she was ready for anything. They had helped out a few poor souls in the last few months. Friends of Donnie needing assistance, but nothing that brought her out of her domain for more than a day. For some reason, she didn't feel comfortable leaving yet. Not until she felt secure with as much knowledge as possible concerning her newfound powers.

"One of those boys is at da door."

Oh, the audacity of those little shits.

Grabbing all three hex bags, she slid them into her large wool sweater pocket on the left side and headed out of the kitchen. What kind of menace were they about to dish out? Not today. Never again.

"We sure will," Mason said as she neared the door.

"We will, what?"

Mason swiveled in her direction, his eyes round with guilt. Oh, she loved this man, but she planned to give him a spanking—she could always turn it naughty in nature after-ward—later for whatever he agreed to. She could see it in his eyes she wouldn't like whatever it was.

Reaching into her right pocket, she grabbed a piece of red licorice, shoving it into her mouth, chewing vehemently as she stared at Mason to respond.

"His cat is missing. I said we'd help."

Her gaze glided to the oldest boy of the trio, Tommy. He was alone, without his pals. But he was the worst one. The one who always had a little lip with her, testing her patience.

"Please. She's been missing since this morning. She always comes back at night for food," Tommy said with just enough pleading to have her convinced he wasn't lying.

Maybe.

"What do you think, Scatter?" Mona asked, reveling in the confused, almost frightened way Tommy leaned back as she spoke to Scatter, who sat by Mason.

Meow.

Growl.

Bozo walked up to her, nudging her thigh, indicating he wanted a bite of licorice, too. He had as much of a sweet tooth as she did.

She ruffled his head, then brought the half-eaten piece of licorice down so he could take a bite. She should've known better. He snatched the rest of it, a smile twinkling in his eyes.

"Okay, fine. We'll help you. Let me get the rest of the gang. I'm sure they won't mind helping either."

Tommy still looked baffled. "That cat meowed and..."

"And?" She prodded when he didn't finish the sentence.

Oh, she knew he thought it odd she was taking the word—or meow—of a cat. The temptation to cackle like a witch tickled in her gut.

But when she caught Mason's gaze, she held it in. He was no fun.

"My sweet Mona, go grab Joe and the guys. I'll ask Tommy a few more questions."

She pulled another licorice out of her pocket, smiling wickedly. "Of course." Then to further bewilder Tommy, she glanced at Scatter and winked. "Why don't you go take a peek outside and see what you can find?"

To her marvelous delight, Scatter listened, trailing around Tommy and dashing out into the night.

Tommy's eyes widened at the sight.

He wanted to treat her like a witch, she'd show him how witchy she could be.

She said nothing else but threw Mason another mischievous smile. He frowned, yet she saw the admiration in his eyes. He didn't like what the boys were doing either. But she also knew he was unhappy about what he discovered in the kitchen.

Bozo followed her as she started up the stairs.

"What happened there?" she heard Tommy say in a soft voice. "I knew something was up with her. Black cat. Weird clothes. Always looking at us funny."

"I don't know what you mean," Mason responded.

She slowed her steps to hear Tommy's response, not even caring if they noticed her slow down.

"She's...a witch," Tommy hissed. "Did you see that cat? She was talking to that cat."

"If you really think so, I'd probably not upset her doing the things you've been doing. You never know what a witch might do." Mason coughed as if he were hiding a laugh. "If she were an actual witch, that is."

Another reason she loved Mason. Putting that boy in his place, sticking up for her, yet trying to help the boy out of a pickle—even if he didn't deserve it. Mason had such a kind heart. How couldn't she love him for it?

It didn't mean she was about to change her mind. The bags in her pocket would be put to good use.

CHUPACABRA...WHAT?

MASON WANTED to spank Mona's ass...then rub it and make it feel better. But first, a good hard spanking for scaring Tommy. Yeah, he was a little shit giving her problems, but there was no need to give the boy nightmares.

"What's your cat's name, and do you have a picture?"

Time to get back to business. As long as he kept Tommy and Mona separated, everything should go smoothly. Hopefully, they found the cat with little effort as well.

Tommy shook his head. "I didn't think to bring a picture. Her name is Bertha."

Mason cocked a brow, a little surprised by the name. "Interesting name."

"She's a fat cat. Big Bertha's her full name. She loves to eat," Tommy said with a chuckle, in a way that made Mason think he gave Bertha more than she should eat on purpose.

"What color is she?"

"Like a weird orange and white mixture. And fat. She's huge. You won't be able to miss her." Tommy said it as if Mason were an idiot.

Mason worked with a few irritating idiots that he ignored every day, he could do the same with this kid.

"Why don't you run home and find a picture of her? Drop it off and we'll start looking for her. Don't worry."

Tommy nodded, then hustled off the porch, sprinting toward the right. He lived three houses down on the opposite side of the street. A shabby looking white fence bordered the property with a garden surrounding the house that looked like it hadn't seen a pair of sheers in years. Although Tommy looked clean and put together, his clothes looked old. It gave Mason enough circumstantial evidence to conclude Tommy's mom didn't have a lot of money.

Just as he ran off the porch to grab the photo, he ran back with it in under two minutes. He either loved that cat, or he had to find it before someone—his mom—realized Bertha was missing. Mason was going with the latter. He knew his mom worked nights, which meant Mason had to find Bertha tonight to keep Tommy out of trouble.

"I'll let you know as soon as we find her."

Mason didn't like to give a false sense of optimism, but it popped out before he could stop himself. By the way Tommy's eyes lit up with appreciation, Mason didn't have the heart to turn his words around.

It was a cat. How hard could it be to find? And Scatter was out there taking a look around. One cat should be able to find another.

As soon as Tommy left, Mason headed upstairs where he found Mona talking to Joe and Donnie in Donnie's room. The same room where the creepy-ass dolls had been stored when he roamed the house as a ghost. He had yet to step foot in the room since that fateful night he turned back into a living, breathing man, and he had no desire to start now.

"How about we have a meeting in the living room about

this?" he said with extra cheeriness to hide the fact he was terrified to walk inside the room.

Mona smiled at him. He turned around before he could witness Donnie or Joe's look—probably one of amusement.

What did they have to be afraid of? Nothing. They were vampires. Strong, heightened sense of smell, night vision. Things to help them sense danger before it even came within feet of them.

Instead of sitting, Mason took a spot near the brown, faded loveseat that Mona loved to curl up on reading her mother's diary. She had found it at a garage sale and couldn't pass it up, even with the few tiny holes on the back and the chipped parts of wood around the bottom pegs. Mona said it needed a little tender loving care, like most things. With a needle and thread, she had the holes fixed, and with a bit of sandpaper and stain, the wooden pegs were like brand new. She loved her new loveseat, along with the brown L-shaped couch she also found at a garage sale. Again, a few little loving tender things had to be done to that as well. It didn't matter she had had perfectly nice furniture in the living room. A white, pristine couch with two decorative chairs that looked like they had never been sat in. The furniture had disturbed her for some reason. After placing a blessing spell on them—to ward off any potential evil—she gave them away without blinking.

When Mona entered the living room, she still wore a sweet smile, patted his cheek, and took a spot on the couch near the place he stood. Joe and Donnie ventured in after her, along with Peter and George, who took a seat on the large brown couch. Donnie and Joe chose to keep standing.

"Scatter's taking a look outside right now," Mason said, then handed Mona a picture of Bertha.

While Tommy had described her as a mixture of orange

and white, she was mostly orange with white paws and a large white patch over her left eye. It made him think a nice name like Jolly Bertha would've been more fun, rather than Big Bertha. The white patch made him think of a pirate.

Mona took a look at the photo, then passed it off to Donnie. "I don't even get why that little shit would come ask us for help."

Joe chuckled at Mona's nickname for Tommy, as did Peter. Donnie smiled but didn't make a sound. George barely reacted with a facial expression. But he was generally like that. Didn't talk much. Didn't express his feelings. Just neutral most of the time. Mason couldn't say he didn't like the guy because he did. After living with these vampires for the last five months, he considered them all friends. He'd do anything for them, just as he knew they'd do anything for him and Mona. To anyone else, it would sound insane. To him, it was his normal life.

They had even suggested after staying with them for the first three weeks they move on, stop taking up space in Mona's home, but Mona wouldn't have it. She insisted they stay. The cabin where they found them had only been a temporary place. The last place they had been living was destroyed by vampire hunters. Very vicious, very deter-mined hunters out to kill them. That alone had Mona demanding they stay. For protection. Donnie had agreed until they figured out a proper solution, one that didn't involve violence. Because even though the hunters meant to maim and kill, Donnie and his friends didn't believe in violence unless it was absolutely necessary.

"I would imagine the *little shit*," Donnie said with a wide smirk, indicating he found Mona more humorous than he first let on, "knows Mason is a detective. He probably figured he'd help."

"It's a cat. How hard can it be to find?" Joe asked, then laughed. "And it's a fat cat based on that photo. How far would it get?"

"Well, we can take a look around outside tonight. If we don't see anything, or smell anything," Mason said, gesturing to his vampire friends who had the amazing skill, "we'll call the local shelters tomorrow. She's not wearing a collar in the picture, but I'll ask Tommy if they had her chipped. As long as someone found her, it should be easy enough."

George made a sound. Almost like a soft grunt. It was honestly the most he had ever contributed when they had a meeting in the living room.

Then Mason saw Donnie nod as if understanding George's odd grunt. Everyone looked toward Donnie. As the leader of the vampires, it didn't surprise him. He was usually the one to take charge and have the final say—at least when it came to him and his friends.

"What is it?" Mason sensed he wouldn't like what Donnie was about to say. An eerie, creepy sensation rattled up his spine.

"As long as a human found her, it should be easy," Donnie replied with a bit of apprehension as if he didn't want to voice it at all.

"Oh, that was all kinds of odd. Be more specific." Mona grabbed another piece of licorice from her pocket and started to vigorously chew on it as if she knew something dooming was about to be laid at their feet.

Donnie shrugged, yet offered a reassuring smile. "I can't say it's anything because I haven't actually seen anything, but I've had the feeling something is close by. Joe mentioned the same kind of odd feeling to me this morning as well."

"What kind of odd feeling?" Mason asked. He only

wanted a nice and simple investigation. Missing cat. Find missing cat. Nothing else needed to be added.

"The kind that doesn't bring anything pleasant."

Mona rolled her eyes and grabbed another licorice. "Enough with the riddles, Donnie. Spit it out before I run out of licorice."

A chuckle slipped out, knowing how true that statement was. No one wanted to see Mona run out of her sweet snacks.

"Have you ever come across a chupacabra before?"

This time a full-blown laugh escaped as Mason stared at Donnie as if he started growing horns on the top of his head. A devil vampire. The very thought was hilarious.

Yet, Donnie didn't laugh. He looked deadly serious.

"I thought they were fictional, first of all," Mason started. "And aren't they found in Puerto Rico or something like that?"

"Well, five months ago, did you think vampires and witches were real?" Donnie countered with a shit-eating grin.

"Oh, he got you there," Mona said with a snicker.

"A chupacabra?" Mason shook his head with disbelief. No way. It couldn't be.

"You have a missing cat. And if you start having more missing animals in the neighborhood, then..." Donnie looked at him deadpan. "Yes, a chupacabra. And we don't get odd feelings for nothing, Mason."

Bozo, who had taken a spot next to Mona, so quiet Mason hadn't even realized he entered the room, perked up and jumped off the couch.

Scatter.

They had sent him out into the neighborhood. In the

dark. With a deadly beast roaming the area that devoured animals.

Bozo had the same thought as him. Before he could stop him, Bozo raced out of the room.

"Oh, I better consult my spells. I don't know how to defeat a chupacabra." Mona then turned to him with fire in her eyes. "Go find Scatter and Bozo now."

"I'll help ya," Petter said, following her out of the room.

"Tell me everything I need to know if it happens to be a chupacabra," Mason said, looking at Donnie. "While we find Scatter and Bozo."

"First things first, we grab weapons before we leave the house."

Not what Mason wanted to hear.

And he'd never forgive himself if something happened to Scatter, even though Mona had asked Scatter to go look around. That cat was his best friend. They'd been through a lot together. He couldn't lose him. And not to a beast.

SCATTER'S JUST A CAT...RIGHT?

HE WALKED SLOWLY, checking his surroundings with an eagle eye. Although his senses were a bit dull at the moment, still smelling a strong odor of ginger. That's what he got for sitting with Mona while she created her potions. She wasn't the neatest either, creating a mess every time she tried to make anything. Some of the ginger had traveled from the counter, down to the floor, and circled the air, even where he lounged on the opposite counter watching her.

Scatter paused when he heard a rustle near the side of the house. The lawn was tall, enough to give him cover from whatever was making the noise. He thought the best place to start looking for Bertha was at her home. Julie, her owner, either didn't care about the upkeep of her house or didn't have the time. She was a single mom raising a child who liked to give Mona too much grief. And if he let his thoughts trail there, he wouldn't get very far. He might not like Tommy, but that had nothing to do with Bertha. He'd never chatted with Bertha before, so he wasn't sure if she had any usual haunts she frequented. Not that he talked with any of the pets in the neighborhood—or even was able to understand them. Regardless, he preferred to stay close to home near Mona and Mason. With those two always finding trouble, he needed to stay close to help them out.

Since Mason had met Mona, his ability to communicate with him had grown stronger. Mason could actually understand him. Which Scatter was eternally grateful for. It made things so much easier. Trying to get his point across with a hiss and a meow didn't cut it.

He started to creep closer when he didn't hear any other sounds, although the hair on his back tingled with...a feeling he hadn't felt in a few months. That same feeling he always got when the malevolent spirit in the house always got close to him and Mason. Thankfully, since Mona had vanquished the evil, he didn't feel that anymore. They were safe and protected in the house.

But he felt it now.

He paused again. Not because he heard more noise—which he didn't—but because the sense he wasn't alone intensified. Glancing around, he didn't see anything. The moonlight shone bright. The tree limbs blew from the slight breeze. The crickets chirped an annoying tune. The streets were empty of cars and people. Nothing was out of place. Yet the feeling increased the longer he stood there.

Perhaps he should return home and get Bozo. Of course, he'd never hear the end of it from the mangy beast. They might like each other, but that didn't always mean they agreed with each other on every issue. Like who got more room on the bed. Before Bozo, he had the entire end of the bed to sleep on. He liked to snuggle near Mona's feet because she didn't toss and turn as much as Mason did. But the moment Bozo joined the picture, he decided he needed to sleep on the bed, too, taking up way too much space. He liked to sleep by Mona's side as well, which pushed Scatter more toward Mason. It wasn't a terrible thing, except when Mason kicked him without realizing it. Scatter refused to sleep on the floor in the nice plushy bed Mona bought months ago.

It was his job to protect them. At first, it had been to protect Mason and keep him safe. As soon as Mona entered the picture, he sensed right away he'd have to protect her, too. And he took his job seriously. No one would hurt them. Not on his watch.

Well, as long as he could help it. He failed—as did Mason—when Mona's aunt entered the picture. Not something he liked to think about either. He was grateful Bozo had joined the mix. Having another protector in the house made his job easier.

So, yeah, maybe he should go home and get Bozo to help.

Scatter hesitated, but it was too late. Whatever had been hiding sprung out toward him. He had no time to react.

———

Mason felt silly walking out of the house wielding an ax, but when Donnie handed it to him, he couldn't say no. Especially with the slight fear in Donnie's eyes. Not much made him nervous, so if the potential thought a chupacabra was in the area concerned him, then it concerned Mason.

"We'll split up. You and Bozo go that way," Donnie said, pointing to the right, "and Joe and I will venture this way." He pointed to his left. "George will hang back at the house, just in case."

Mason followed Donnie's hand, shivering, as he found nothing but darkness to the left. They lived at the end of the street with fields surrounding the house. The street lamp illuminated the area only so far, and the direction Donnie pointed was one area it didn't extend to. Yep. Mason was completely okay with that plan. They had the intensified eyesight. It made the most sense.

"Got it."

Then he and Bozo headed down the small walkway to the sidewalk. He was thankful Bozo hadn't run off. He had waited for him on the porch as if he knew better than to leave without him.

"Where do we think Scatter headed first?"

Growl.

Mason nodded. "Yeah, I think so, too."

They turned right, but instead of checking the houses close to theirs, they continued until they made it to Tommy's house. The most logical conclusion where Scatter would've started his search. At the scene of the crime.

If there was a crime.

A chupacabra. Mason still had trouble wrapping his mind around it.

Yet, the ax in his right hand said it was a strange possibility.

Would it be hard to kill? Donnie said they weren't that large, but big enough to do damage. About three to four feet long with a sharp, scaly back, long claws, and oh, yeah, they sucked the blood of their victims. Like a vampire. Which was one reason Donnie said they could sense something evil nearby.

Not good. Not good at all.

Mason approached Tommy's house, glancing around the darkened yard. It was hard to see much as the house was plunged in black. He could only assume Tommy's mom wasn't home from work yet. But where was Tommy? Why were all the lights out? The streetlight sprinkled part of the front lawn, but not enough to reach the house.

Growl.

Mason glanced down at Bozo and nodded. Yeah, he sensed something was off as well. The air felt charged with...a freaky energy. A sense of foreboding that was teetering on the edge of knocking him on his ass.

He didn't like the feeling coursing through his veins at all. Although he wanted Mona safe and far from harm, he wished she were right next to him. They always walked into danger together, and it felt odd without her by his side.

Venturing closer to the house, he kept his eyes peeled, making furtive glances, trying not to miss anything, even the smallest clue. Bozo stuck close by, sniffing the ground, doing his own detecting as well.

The ax felt heavy, ladened, as he continued to inch forward.

He felt more comfortable with a gun. He had even told Donnie so. But apparently, it wouldn't be good enough to take down a chupacabra. It would be hard for the bullets to penetrate the thick, leathery skin. Which was why Donnie had shoved the ax in his hand and said, "Aim for the head. Chop it clean off."

Oh, yeah. Sounded so easy.

Well, he was prepared to use the ax, but he had his gun strapped to his hip for extra protection. One could never be too prepared.

"Scatter," Mason whispered.

Nothing answered back but the brisk slap of the wind.

Why couldn't this have happened during the daytime? The night added a layer of spookiness he didn't want to deal with. Especially the day before Halloween. Tommy's mom, Julie, liked to decorate, as most of the other houses on the street did. Two skeletons were lounging on the steps of the porch, one on each side. One even looked like it had a shit-eating grin, saying, "Come closer, I dare ya." Nope. Mason wouldn't go near if he didn't have to, even if it was only a plastic prop.

In the flower garden surrounding the porch, two pumpkins sat staring at him with their grotesque looking faces. Both looked downright mean and ready to chop his head off with one bite. By the looks of them, Tommy had fun carving them. A little choppy, but quite creative. Mason was thankful they weren't lit up at the moment by a candle. It would've only added to the spooky factor.

Julie had also hung a few fun Halloween decals to the front windows. Not too many decorations, but enough to say Halloween was a holiday they enjoyed.

Mona loved the holiday. While she didn't decorate the outside, the inside of the house looked like a Halloween bomb had exploded. Fake spider webs hanging here and there. Little knick-knacks splattered around each corner. She practically screamed with glee when she found the sign 'witches haven' at a local artist shop. She proudly hung it in the kitchen. Of course, the large coffin in the foyer added just the right touch. It would freak out a few kids tomorrow when they knocked on the door for their treats.

"Scatter," Mason whispered harshly, looking around the yard.

Again, nothing answered back.

"Shit, Scatter. Where are you?"

A loud creaking sound had him jumping and turning back toward the house. Light from inside the house spilled out into the front yard.

"Did you find her?"

Mason willed his heart to slow down, irritated at himself for letting the kid make him jump.

"Not yet. But we're on the case. Don't worry. Stay inside while we search." *Because I don't want your blood to be sucked dry and killed by a chupacabra.* Not that he'd ever voice that, no matter how cruel the kid could be to Mona.

Tommy nodded, then his eyes glided to the ax dangling from his hand. "Why are you carrying an ax?"

"This?" Mason chuckled, a mixture of embarrassment and fright. How did he explain this? "In case Bertha's stuck... in something. Always good to be prepared."

Tommy eyed him critically as if he didn't believe him. Hell, Mason wouldn't believe him either. It sounded stupid. But hey, he didn't always think fast on his feet, this being a prime example.

"Go back inside, Tommy. I'll bring Bertha home as soon as I find her."

Hopefully alive.

More unspoken words he'd never utter.

Tommy hesitated, then shut the door without another word.

"Scatter!" This time he didn't whisper. There was also an edge of irritation there. He needed Scatter to pop out right this minute. For reassurance, and most importantly, his sanity. It was starting to come unhinged.

Growl.

Mason jerked his attention to Bozo, who had ventured closer to the side of the house. The dangerous vibes he felt started to vibrate even harder as he approached him.

Growl.

Grabbing his phone and switching on the light, he needed to see with his own eyes what Bozo just communicated.

It was hard to tell with the tiny light from his phone and the darkness swirling around them like a twister hell-bent on destruction. But as soon as he touched the few blades of grass, he knew it wasn't a lie.

His fingers were wet.

With blood.

But whose?

Bertha's...or Scatter's?

Or shit. Both.

MAKE IT WEAK

MONA STIFFENED when Peter laid a hand over hers. She was trying to find a spell to defeat a chupacabra. This was her home, her neighborhood. While she might not be the most liked on the street, she wasn't about to allow an evil monster to come into her space and hurt people. Or cats. Or anybody —even the little shits who got on her nerves.

"You won't be finding a spell in there."

Well, Peter obviously didn't know her. She was tenacious and downright stubborn at times. She would find something.

"I will."

He removed his hand from hers and smiled. "I like your persistence." Then his smile dipped. "Chupacabras are strong. Very hard to kill. Their skin is coated like leather, so it be hard to penetrate. You gotta cut their heads off."

Mona grimaced, a bloody image flashing through her already frazzled mind. Blood spatter coating the walls, making a haphazard pattern. More blood gushing from the neck, spurting all over the floor. The head, now detached, falling and rolling to the floor. Of course, because her imagination could be very vivid, the head stopping no more than an inch from her, its beady, evil eyes staring up at her, saying, "Why'd you kill me? I only wanted to drain your blood. No biggie."

Yeah, no thanks. She didn't like that mental picture. She'd find a spell and potion that would kill it with less blood involved. Hopefully.

"I thought you said you were going to help me, Peter." Mona grabbed her bag of red licorice sitting on the opposite counter and opened it. Stashing a few pieces in her pocket, knowing she'd need it, she also put one in her mouth and started to absently chew it.

"I am."

Mona rolled her eyes as she chuckled, an idea suddenly popping up. "Grab me some of those chamomile leaves, please."

He eyed her funnily, then snatched the tall glass jar filled to the rim with chamomile leaves. Mona liked to be prepared for any spell, at any time. Mason had thought she was overdoing it when she started to search for and obtain all sorts of ingredients. But this way she was stocked and ready for every spell she deciphered in her mother's journal. One could never be too prepared. That was her motto. Look, it was coming in handy now. Although, she did enjoy chamomile tea on occasion. She was still trying to get Mason to enjoy tea. Coffee, coffee, coffee. The man didn't drink anything else in the morning, sometimes even in the afternoon. He even enjoyed a cup at night. If she drank coffee at night, she'd be bouncing off the walls until the sun rose for another day.

"Chamomile is meant to relax." Peter's brows scrunched inward as if he were trying very hard to follow her train of thought.

"Exactly. You say this creature is strong. We need to make it weak."

"Ah, it be easier to kill it then."

Mona shivered. She did not want to be around when one of them decapitated the creature.

"What else ya be needing?"

She grabbed another licorice from her pocket, inhaling the first one, then started to rattle off all the ingredients she'd need. She wasn't one for stereotypes and playing a role, but it amused and made her giggle every time she pulled her small black caldron out to make a potion.

She was a witch. Witches created magic. They used black caldrons to do so. So she did as well.

"Grab me some of those lavender stems. I also need that jar of rose oil."

Tossing in everything, she scrunched up the leaves first with a wooden mallet she found at a garage sale this past summer, then added the various liquids. After getting the perfect texture, she nodded to Peter.

"Grab me one of those small jars behind you."

Peter twisted and picked up a tiny glass jar that could hold about 20 ml of whatever she so choose. He set the jar near her, where she then carefully poured most of the mixture she had created into the jar. What could she say? She was new to this witchy business. She had yet to make a potion with just the right amount of ingredients to fill up one jar.

"I need one more."

Peter offered a half-grin as he grabbed another jar.

She might not get the portions correct, but that didn't mean she was about to waste anything she made. So, she filled up the second jar as well, which, unfortunately, only went up about halfway.

Yeah, she was definitely a work in progress. Practice, practice, practice. The more potions she made, the better she'd be. Soon, she'd be able to make one and fill up a jar with no leftovers, or a potion for three jars full, without room to spare.

Soon.

Maybe.

When did she ever get anything right in life?

She smiled as she popped a cork into each jar. She might not get most things right in life, making one bad mistake after another, but she never gave up, and that had to count for something.

"Why ya be putting it in a glass jar? Why not one of those bag thingamajigs you make?"

Mona always loved the way Peter talked, especially with his adorable accent. Not quite Irish, although it reminded her a bit of it. Not quite Jamaican, but she swore she heard a few intonations as if he were. Not quite Scottish. It was difficult to pinpoint exactly where he came from. Although she had gotten a brief background on them, it felt intrusive to ask more personal questions. She did, however, know Peter was the third youngest vampire of the group. About two hundred years old. Yep, real young.

She still had a hard time processing that information when she thought about it. Here he was, helping her, talking to her, as if he weren't over two hundred years old.

"Well, with the bag, the contents always stay inside, still performing its magic. They don't need to come out. But with certain spells, you need the potion to touch the recipient. Hence, the jar. We throw it at the chupacabra, it'll break, spreading the spell like we need it to. Someone with good skills because mine are nonexistent." Mona shrugged and laughed. It was true. She hated sports in school but always suffered through because, well, she had no choice. But no one ever liked it when she was on their team. She had two left feet and a terrible aim.

"Once it hits the chupacabra, it'll spill the contents all over it. It should weaken it for one of you strong, powerful men to kill it."

Peter's brow rose. "And if we miss?"

Mona inhaled deeply. "Don't miss. I don't think I have enough pig's blood to make another dose."

Another reason she didn't want to make it again was she hated using the pig's blood in any potion. Gross! Which was why she didn't keep a lot on hand. And those poor pigs. To have to donate their blood. She wasn't exactly sure how Mason always got it for her. She never asked. He never supplied the answer.

Blood was disgusting. So, yeah, the thought of decapitating this thing was not something she wanted to be a part of.

"I hope this works."

Mona's heart started to beat faster at the thought of seeing a spurt of blood. "Me, too."

Then she grabbed another licorice and shoved it into her mouth. She'd consume the entire bag within minutes if she wasn't careful.

Time to recite the spell to make the potion work. Her voice filled the room as she held both potion bottles tightly in her hands.

You think you're strong, you're not.
A splash of purple, to calm your senses.
A dash of yellow, to relax your tresses.
Mash it with a bit of rose, to reduce your defenses.
You think you're strong, you're not.

"That be it, then?"

Mona glanced at Peter, hoping this worked. She was flying by the seat of her pants. She hoped this would be it.

"Yep. Would I steer you wrong?"

Peter gave her a dubious look. Yeah, she deserved that. But when in doubt, be confident. Confidence never steered her wrong yet.

NO, FORMER GHOST

"Okay, let's stay calm, Bozo. It's all good. Everything's good," Mason whispered as he continued to rub his fingers together, feeling the icky sensation of blood.

But whose blood?

He glanced up when Bozo whimpered. Yeah, he agreed. This didn't look good.

Either Scatter was hurt, which would break his heart and kill Mona to pieces—in fact, he wasn't even sure how he'd tell Mona if something terrible happened to Scatter—or Bertha was hurt, and he didn't relish the idea of telling a kid, even if he did act like a little shit at times, that his cat wasn't coming home.

"It's all good. It has to be." Then he wiped the blood off his fingers by brushing his hand against the grass. And struck something sharp.

"Shit."

Pulling his hand away, he felt the trickle of blood before he saw it leaking from the side of his middle finger.

Great. And now he was bleeding.

Growl.

"I'm fine. Everything's fine. We're fine. It's all going to be fine."

If wolves could talk, Mason knew Bozo would've probably called him a neurotic idiot or something. Because he sounded like one. Repeating the word fine or good wouldn't make the situation so.

Shining his phone down toward the grass again, he tried to find whatever had cut him. Not too deep, but enough to draw blood. Which sucked, since he had nothing to stop the slow trickle. So, he did what he had to do. Wiped it on his pants—something he knew Mona would give him hell for later. She wasn't a huge fan of blood but tolerated it. They had to buy a separate refrigerator where Donnie and the guys could store their supply. Mona didn't like to see it every time she opened the fridge. And when they drank it—because hey, these were refined vampires—they drank it out of mugs and glasses that concealed what was inside. Mona bought them a huge supply of different colored glasses so they had variety and style as they drank their liquid. Mason always chuckled when he saw Joe drinking out of the tumbler that was solid black and had the words 'Too cool to drool' written in bright red.

A shiver rippled down his spine the second his eyes hit what he was looking for. He set his ax down. When he picked up the long, curved quill, another terrifying shiver rushed down his spine.

It was black, not too thick in size, but also not super thin. The end was very sharp, something his hand could attest to. Like the point of a needle ready to pierce the fabric with determination.

"Do we have any porcupines in the area?"

If wolves could express a mocking face, Bozo would be

the best at it. Even in the dark, Mason could feel his brow rising as if saying, "You did not just say that."

Yeah, it was a dumb comment, but it was better than thinking there was a real-life chupacabra in their neighborhood.

But it also explained the other drops of blood. Someone was injured by the quill—or quills. Or even claws.

Again, but who?

"Come on. We need to update the gang on this. Everyone needs to know what we're up against. It's not looking good."

Mason started to turn around and jumped back a step. Tommy stood close to him with a metal baseball bat in his hand.

"What's not looking good?"

"Go back inside, Tommy. When I find Bertha, I'll bring her home." Unless she was mangled into tiny pieces by a chupacabra. Because then he was shit out of luck. There was nothing in this world that could make him let a child witness something like that. Although he didn't believe in lying, he'd lie to Tommy that he couldn't find Bertha, rather than tell him she was demolished by a monster.

"I want to help." His stance went rigid. "You ignored what I asked."

And he'd continue to do so. Some little teenage brat wasn't going to tell him what to do. He'd come across difficult adults in his life, because that's generally who he dealt with when it came to arresting people for violent crimes, but a kid talking back to him? Not listening to him? That was new.

"What do you think you're going to do with that bat?"

Tommy smirked. "What are you going to do with the ax?"

"I already answered that." And his answer would have to suffice because he wasn't repeating it.

"She's my cat and I want to help."

Mason didn't have time for this. He had to find Scatter.

"Fine. But stay behind me." Just in case a chupacabra suddenly jumped in front of them. Not that he'd ever voice that.

Mason quietly slid the quill into his pocket, although careful not to scratch himself. He imagined the sharp object could pierce him through his pants. Then he picked up his ax and headed out of Tommy's front yard as he slid his phone back into his other pocket. Tommy was close on his heels the entire time, with Bozo on his other side.

He wasn't sure where to go from here. He couldn't exactly find Donnie to tell him about the quill and let Tommy overhear everything. He also couldn't go home and tell Mona—and show up with Tommy. That wouldn't go over well either.

So, he headed across the street to the empty field next to their house, hoping to find Scatter alive and well. And Bertha, of course.

"Is she really a witch?" Tommy's voice penetrated the dark night with a mixture of confidence and terror all mingled in a voice on the verge of puberty.

Mason wasn't exactly sure how old Tommy was, but if he had to guess, at least thirteen. He was in that awkward stage where his voice dipped high and low, especially high when he was agitated. And in the last thirty minutes, he had a lot to be agitated about.

"Ask yourself, if you really believe that, then why are so mean to her?" Mason stopped and twisted around to look him in the eyes. "In my experience, bullies are mean for one reason. Because they're not happy with themselves."

"I'm not a bully."

Mason shrugged. He wasn't about to get into it with the kid. Because, although he was only a kid and Mona was a grown adult, he did bully her. Writing mean messages on the sidewalk. Egging the house. Nobody saw him—or his friends—do it, but Mason wasn't dumb. The kid did it. Little things here and there that made Mona so upset, she made a potion that would make Tommy regret every little nasty thing he ever did or said to her.

They continued to walk in silence. Mason walked slow, checking out the entire area for any signs of Scatter, Bertha, and unfortunately, a chupacabra. There were a few trees scattered around here and there, but only one large tree that stood out amongst the rest. The remaining area was filled with long, tall grass that came to almost his knees. Since he had never seen—hell, even believed in—a chupacabra, he couldn't be sure if the creature was small enough to be hiding in the tall brush.

"My mom's boyfriend is a jackass."

Mason stopped and turned toward Tommy again. Interesting change of topic.

"Sorry to hear that."

And it made Mason wonder just how much of a jackass he was. Maybe he'd have Donnie and the guys do a bit of recon at night and see exactly what Tommy was talking about. With a keen sense of hearing and night vision, it'd be easy for them to find out what was going on. Tommy's mom, Julie, was a nice lady. He'd chatted with her a few times. He didn't like to think of anyone being treated poorly in his neighborhood, even Tommy himself.

Tommy looked down at his feet. "I don't even know why she likes him." Then he looked up. "I don't mean to act...tell Mona I'm sorry."

A slow grin emerged on Mason's face. "I think you should tell her yourself." Oh, boy, should he, otherwise he'd be having a terrible Halloween night sitting on the toilet.

Tommy jerked his head to the right, clutching the baseball bat tighter. "Did you hear that?"

Mason followed his line of sight, unable to see anything. He wasn't sure what he heard. A bit of rustling in the grass. Maybe a small animal. Maybe the wind. It wasn't a strong breeze, but enough to blow his hair now and again.

"Stick close to me." Mason tightened the grip on the ax and turned to offer Tommy a reassuring smile that everything would be okay.

"Whoa, dude."

"What?" Mason's heart started to pound. Something had to be behind him by the terror echoing in the kid's eyes.

"Your eyes. There glowing like a weird blue. Are you a witch, too?"

Well, shit.

Not a good time for his body to be acting like a ghost, or whatever the hell it was doing. His eyes had only glowed one other time. When they found the cabin in the woods where Donnie and his friends were hiding.

Why were they doing it again? And in front of Tommy?

When in doubt, go with the truth. Because Tommy wasn't likely to believe any lie he would come up with. Hell, he wouldn't believe this either.

"No, former ghost."

GLOWING CONTACTS

As soon as they stepped outside, Mona shivered. Sure, there was a slight chill in the air. It was the end of October, winter almost rearing its ugly head. But also because of what they were about to do. She hated this kind of thing hitting so close to home.

It always came back to this house and bad, creepy things happening around it. George would stay back at the house, in case the creature decided to approach. Perhaps Peter should stay back as well. Being alone was never smart. Of course, that would put her alone, and she knew Peter would never allow that. Once Mason found out, he wouldn't be a happy camper either. No sense in arguing with either man. Plus, she didn't want to be alone if she came across the chupacabra. Yeah, sure. She had grabbed a weapon. Donnie and the guys had a lot of weapons. They had even insisted she and Mason stock up their supplies, ready for anything.

It had been a choice between an ax or a samurai sword. She opted for the sword, as it was lighter than the ax and much cooler to carry. Hello. Samurai sword. Way cooler. Not to mention, they said the best way to kill the chupacabra was to chop its head off. A sword would make it so much easier. Not that she had any intention of getting close to the beast. She would leave that to the brawny men. Yep. She had no problem with that whatsoever.

"Which way?" she asked Peter, knowing he'd use his senses to figure out where everyone went. Hopefully. The last five months had been about preparing for this sort of thing, not actually using their abilities in a situation.

Peter paused, turning his head left and right. Then he pointed left. "Donnie and Joe went that way." His hand then gestured right. "Mason and Bozo went that way."

So, which way should they go? And with only one full bottle of potion.

"I'd like to find Mason first. Make sure he found Scatter."

She always felt better with Mason by her side when they were walking into danger as well. Together, they always did better. Nothing could hurt them. At least, nothing had yet.

Peter nodded, and they headed down the few porch steps to the right.

It didn't take long to find them. Tommy was with Mason and being loud while they stood in the field close to their house.

"Dude, you're a witch. Ghosts don't exist."

Mona laughed. Did Tommy even hear what he just said? That made no sense. Witches shouldn't exist either, not if ghosts didn't.

Tommy jumped at her laughter. His eyes were large and round, his hand shaking where he held a baseball bat. Why was he holding a baseball bat? Geez, she hadn't even done her best cackle. Why was he so frightened? She only laughed a little.

Then she glanced at Mason, whose eyes were glowing a

bright blue. Just like they had a few months ago right before they found their vampire friends.

"What's going on here?"

Tommy took a step back. "He said he's a former ghost. But you're all witches."

Mona gave Mason a pointed glare. He simply shrugged with a crooked smile. Yeah, she understood that smile. What was he supposed to tell the kid? His eyes were glowing a brilliant blue. It was kind of hard to explain. No explanation was going to go over well, so why not try the truth? That sure didn't work.

"Actually, he's a vampire," Mona said with a wicked smile as she pointed at Peter, who sighed and shook his head in exasperation. Well, when in Rome, and all that jazz.

"You're all crazy." Tommy took another step back.

"Only on Wednesdays because that's garbage day and I hate that they always make a mess and don't get every piece of garbage into the truck. Here I am, picking up after them when I shouldn't have to." Seriously. It annoyed her to no end. Everyone knew to keep their distance until she got all her irritation out of her system on garbage days.

"You're carrying a sword. Why?"

Mona glanced at her sword, then glanced at the baseball bat in Tommy's hand. "Why are you carrying a bat?"

Besides Mason's glowing eyes, she wasn't sure what else Mason had told the kid and why he was even searching with him. They had a potential chupacabra in the area. Not a good idea to have the kid tagging along, even if she didn't like the little shit.

"Because he's carrying an ax," Tommy said, gesturing toward Mason, who shrugged again. "So, what's with the sword?"

"Well, if you must know," Mona started, hoping she'd

come up with something good to explain, because it wasn't something she really could explain, "I don't like the dark. I also don't particularly like you, but I do like cats. Well, I like Scatter, who is a cat. I didn't use to like cats. So, I guess I do now since I like Scatter. Anyway, I'm getting off track. I want to find Bertha, which means being outside in the dark, and I feel better with a weapon."

There. That sounded like a semi-plausible reason.

Tommy nodded slowly as if buying her excuse.

"And his eyes are glowing, why?"

"Contacts. Duh." Mona rolled her eyes like she couldn't believe he didn't know that.

Yay for her for thinking so quick on her feet.

"Contacts? Glowing contacts?" Tommy's eyes narrowed. "So, why weren't they glowing when I first came outside and saw him. They just started."

"Hello? They're glowing contacts. They take a while to warm up. Like glow in the dark stickers."

Mason whimpered as if he were trying to suppress his laughter. Because seriously, the words coming out of her mouth right now were ridiculous. She wouldn't blame Tommy for not believing her. She didn't believe her either.

Tommy nodded again. "Okay. You're still weird."

"And you're still a little shit."

Tommy jerked, and Mona felt bad for saying something like that to him. He was only a kid. She was an adult, and she should act like it.

"Look, Tommy, I know we don't get along, but I want to find Bertha. I don't think you should be out here. It's dark, it's creepy, and I already have enough to deal with." Like a blood-sucking chupacabra.

"Well, you have a sword. The dark shouldn't be as creepy

with such a cool weapon." Tommy's eyes lit up with appreciation. "It's seriously cool."

Mona smiled as she lifted the sword. "It is, isn't it?

"Okay, then. We have that settled," Mason interjected, looking at Tommy. "Go back home. As soon as we find Bertha, we'll bring her home."

Tommy hesitated, then nodded once. "Fine. Please find her."

Then he turned around and all but ran out of the field and across the street to his house. Maybe she wasn't the only one afraid of the dark. Not that she was afraid of the dark. As long as Mason was by her side, not much frightened her.

"Contacts? Really?" Mason chuckled.

"Telling him you're a former ghost? Really?" she countered.

"I didn't know how to explain it." Mason's eyes softened. "It was a good excuse. We do have a problem, though."

His eyes suddenly started to glow even brighter.

Oh, yeah. They had a problem if his eyes were an indicator of it. Maybe he was a dang-o-meter for them. His eyes giving them a sign danger was near.

"What be the problem?" Peter asked.

"We found blood near Tommy's house. But no sign of Bertha...or Scatter."

"He's a smart cat." Mona had to believe that or she would go insanely crazy. Tommy would never leave his house if he saw her behavior.

"We'll find him, and this chupacabra bastard." Mona lifted the small potion bottle. "A potion to weaken it. Let's do this."

"Together."

Mason held out his hand.

Yep. Together.

They could always accomplish anything together.

FROM LIMB TO LIMB

SCATTER THOUGHT about hissing to get his point across, but it wouldn't do anything but make the dumb fat cat climb farther up the tree.

He found Bertha.

Up in a tree.

Yeah, sure, he was a cat. But he didn't do idiotic things like climb a tree and not know how to get down. He thought things out before doing something. Most of the time.

Of course, he wasn't *just* a cat either. So, he knew better than to scramble up a tree. But he had to give Bertha credit. She did it for a reason. He was also curious how she did it. She truly was a fat cat.

There was something out here with them. Scatter simply wasn't sure what it was. He felt a presence. A malevolent one. He sensed it was close. One reason he fled Tommy's yard after the stupid rabbit jumped out at him. He would never admit to anyone that a rabbit scared him. Nope. Not even a little bit. And he knew the rabbit hadn't done it delib-erately. Something else had scared the small animal, which made it jump toward him. Which made him flee because he knew whatever it was wasn't friendly.

Instead of running back to Mona and Mason, he kept on searching for Bertha, where he found her up in a tree behind their house.

No matter how many times he meowed at her to come down, she wouldn't. He certainly didn't want to climb up to get her. Once up there, he had no idea how he'd get her down besides pushing her off the tree limb. That sounded cruel. But he was tempted. They needed to leave. He could feel the presence getting closer. The way Bertha meowed now and again, she felt it, too.

It's too bad he couldn't communicate with her. While he might look like a cat, act like a cat, meow like a cat, he couldn't speak to other cats where they heard his words. Not like Mason did.

It would sure come in handy right now, though, if she could.

Meow.

The hair on the back of Bertha prickled, standing at attention.

Okay. Either she didn't like the way he meowed at her—very nicely, he thought—or that eerie presence was coming closer.

He couldn't leave her alone to find Mason. He'd never forgive himself if something happened to her. Like Mona, he wasn't a fan of the neighborhood kids, but that didn't mean he'd wish ill on one of their pets. That would be beyond cruel.

Rustling from the side of the house drifted his way.

Something was coming.

Not good.

That left him with only one choice because fleeing was not an option. Not this time.

Digging his claws in for traction, he scrambled up the tree until he was right next to Bertha. She scooted away from him, meowing as if afraid of him. Seriously. She had far worse things to worry about than him right now.

But her movement put her closer to the tree trunk rather than dangling from a limb. Which helped to hide her better.

He needed to hide, too. But as he crept closer and closer to Bertha, the more she kept trying to scoot back. Then she looked up.

Oh, no.

Nope.

Don't do that, he thought. *Don't climb even farther up the tree.*

He stopped moving, wondering what the next best move would be.

The rustling from the side of the house grew louder.

He was running out of time.

———

"Something be back here. I heard it," Peter whispered as they crept toward the back of the house.

Mason didn't doubt Peter. Hello, he was a vampire with acute hearing. Of course, he didn't doubt him. He simply didn't relish the idea of walking toward danger, especially with Mona by his side. And yes, they always did better together, but that didn't mean he wanted her walking toward danger. He'd rather have her sitting inside away from all harm.

But his sweet Mona would never sit idly by while everyone else did the dirty work. He smiled as he glanced at her, a piece of licorice dangling from her mouth, her lips moving in a circle as she chewed it. The large-ass sword gripped tightly in her hands. Oh yeah, his sweet Mona would never sit back and let the rest of them handle the problem. She would always want to be in the thick of things.

She was adorable as hell. It didn't matter they were walking into potential danger. Nothing could dim her beauty.

As they turned the corner, his heart beating like he was zapped by an electrical current, he expected a large, scaly beast to jump out and attack them.

Except nothing happened.

Their house was surrounded by fields. Nothing but tall grass—because he only mowed so far—and a few trees stared back at them.

"I thought you said you heard something, Peter," Mason said quietly, in case the beast was hiding.

"I did."

Then Mason heard it.

Meow.

Meow.

Two very distinct meows. One full of fright and more feminine. He had no idea how he could distinguish that as a normal meow from a cat.

The other meow he heard had the worry swimming inside his veins disappearing. Because he would always recognize Scatter's voice.

"Where are you, Scatter?" He started to look around, catching the relief in Mona's eyes.

Meow.

He looked up at the large tree near them and chuckled.

Sitting tucked in a bundle of limbs near the top was

Bertha, who looked very frightened and out of her element. Near her and not looking very amused was Scatter.

"How'd you get up there?"

Meow.

Yeah, that was a dumb question. He'd have to agree. Mason figured the better question would be, why'd he go up there? Because the moment Scatter found Bertha, he should've come looking for him to help get her down.

Before he could ask the better question, Scatter spoke again.

The hair on his arms stood to attention, his spine shivering with unease.

"What he say?" Peter whispered, knowing whatever Scatter had said wasn't good.

"Something else is near, but he hasn't seen what."

Mona stepped closer to the tree. "Get Bertha down from there, Scatter. I'll take her home and you brawny men can take care of the chupacabra."

Mason almost laughed out loud when he swore he saw Scatter roll his eyes. Of course, he had to have imagined it. First, Scatter was a cat—albeit a cat he could fully understand as if he were using words when meowing at him. Second, it was dark out. The moon helped provide a small amount of light, but not nearly enough.

"Here, hold my ax. I'll climb up there and get her." Mason handed the ax to Mona, kissed her lips because he felt like it, and then looked up at the tree.

He couldn't remember the last time he climbed a tree. Memories from before were so distant, they didn't even feel real at times. Like his life hadn't officially started until the moment he met Mona.

"I'll give ya a boost." Peter set down the machete he had

taken along for the trip and cupped his hands for Mason to step into.

Good idea. Because without jumping—and probably looking like an idiot—he'd never be able to get a good hold of the first limb.

He knew Peter was strong, but he hesitated before finally putting a foot into his hands. He barely had time to adjust his weight when Peter lifted him like he was nothing more than a stick lying on the ground. Damn. He was more than strong.

Mason grabbed the limb, using Peter and the tree to get his footing perfect, and within seconds, was sitting in the tree. He never thought about heights and whether or not they concerned him. Looking down—not too high up—he decided he wasn't a huge fan. Or maybe it was the thought of grabbing Bertha, a cat already terrified, and trying to get her down from the tree without her clawing and tearing him apart.

Well, it had to be done. He knew Mona would have a nice spell and potion to heal his wounds a lot faster than letting nature take its course. One nice thing about dating a witch.

He managed to climb from limb to limb until he was within reaching distance of Bertha.

"Shh, Bertha. It's okay. I'm here to take you home. You want to go home, right? Tommy's been worried."

Meow.

Although her meow sounded scared, he swore he also heard a hint of relief.

"We can do this, sweet girl. Together." Just like he and Mona did all the time.

Reaching carefully toward her, he was surprised when she didn't put up too much of a fight. Cradling her as best as he could, he glanced at Scatter, who sat on a limb above them.

"Do you need help, too?"

Meow.

Okay. Message received. Scatter did not need help. But Scatter shouldn't blame him for asking. It's not like he'd ever climbed a tree before. At least, not that Mason was aware.

As best as he could, without jostling Bertha too much, he climbed back down. He knew he frightened Bertha when he jumped down from the last limb. Her claws digging into his chest was a good indication. Damn, it hurt. But right now wasn't the time to be crying out in pain. The less noise they made, the better chance the chupacabra wouldn't attack—hopefully.

He handed Bertha to Mona, where he was surprised to see Bertha settle in her arms as if she found her new home. And Mona said she wasn't a fan of animals. They were definitely a fan of hers.

"I gave Peter the potion. Don't miss."

Then she was off. A cat nestled on one side with a samurai sword dangling from the other. Odd picture, but so Mona. Beautiful and unique and full of spirit.

"Here." Peter handed him his ax. "We should find Joe and Donnie."

Mason nodded, wholeheartedly agreeing with that. Three strong vampires and little ol' him. Yeah, he'd feel better with three strong vampires against a chupacabra.

He glanced down at his feet when he felt something brush against his leg. Scatter gazed up at him with what he swore was relief.

Yeah, he was relieved as well Scatter wasn't hurt. From climbing down the tree and finding him before the chupacabra did.

Except, whose blood did he find?

A rustling noise behind him had his body tingling with unease once again.

"Whatever you do, Mason, don't be turning around. Stay still."

Not what he wanted to hear.

Shit.

WE'RE FRIENDS NOW

"You are such a sweet thing. Why are you living with Tommy?"

Well, Mona knew it wasn't the cat's fault. She had no choice, and technically Tommy's mom was her owner.

And okay. Maybe Mona could try harder when it came to the kids in the neighborhood. She did tend to go out of her way to make it seem like she was odd and perhaps a witch—which she really was. It didn't mean she had to scare the kids into thinking it was true. It was just so easy.

She had to suppress a laugh as her thoughts swirled around.

But if she stopped her witchy ways, maybe they would too.

Returning his cat would be a nice olive branch to make amends.

His house was dark as she approached it. So odd. She knew his mother was working, something she did most nights, but why wouldn't Tommy have a few lights on for himself?

She stared at the door, wondering how to knock. Bertha

was on her left side, and she wasn't going to put her down. The samurai sword was in her right hand, and there was no way she would be putting that down either. No way she'd give the chupacabra a chance to attack her without a weapon.

So, she kicked the door in lieu of a knock. Lightly, of course. Her intention was not to scare the bejesus out of the kid.

A few—long—seconds later, the door swung open. His eyes, which had been filled with a bit of fright, relaxed when he saw it was her. Interesting. Who else would he be afraid of? She thought she was the only one that gave the kid problems.

"You found her!" Tommy took Bertha from Mona's arm, snuggling the cat before Bertha had enough and leaped from his arms.

She ran out of Mona's view, but as long as Tommy didn't have any windows or other doors open, Bertha would be safe inside.

"Thank you."

She could tell by the way he swallowed hard before speaking that he struggled to voice the words. Yet, he did.

"You're welcome." Her feet itched to walk away, but her heart told her she couldn't. "Look, Tommy, I think we got off on the wrong foot. Probably from the moment I moved in. I know you think I'm weird, and I think you're a little shit. But I don't want to be at odds with you or anybody in the neighborhood."

He looked taken aback by her words, yet she could see he was also relieved. As if he didn't want to be at odds with her either.

"I'm sorry for being a little shit."

Mona smiled. "I'm sorry for being...a witch...to you."

Tommy's eyes narrowed as if contemplating those words.

"Why are all the lights out?"

She shouldn't tempt fate. They were apologizing to each other. So, changing the conversation sounded like the best course of action. Plus, she was curious. Her curiosity could be considered a fault because it got her into too much trouble sometimes.

He shrugged. "Just are."

Hmm. He was hiding something. But what? And did she have to find out?

"Come on, Tommy. We're friends. You can tell me the truth."

He shuffled his feet, looking at the ground. "I don't like it when my mom's boyfriend comes over when she's not here. If the lights are on, he thinks she's home and doesn't leave when he sees she's not. If the lights are out, it means my mom's not home and I'm at a friend's house."

"Why don't you like him?"

Tommy looked up. "He's an asshole. Can't stand him."

"Well, we're friends now, right?"

She had no idea what she was doing here, but although she didn't get along with Tommy, she wasn't cruel to him. Yeah, okay, the fun Halloween bags she made earlier tonight would creep into the cruelty stage. She realized that now. But if someone else was picking on Tommy, someone who made the kid keep all the lights out to trick him into thinking he wasn't home, that wasn't okay.

"Sure," Tommy replied, shrugging.

"You turn on those lights. Play some video games. Do whatever it is you do when your mom is working. If he shows up, giving you problems, you call me."

"What are you going to do?"

Well, she had three hex bags just waiting to be used now.

"Have a nice friendly chat with him, of course. Nothing nefarious."

Tommy glanced at the sword in her hand. "You plan on carrying that around everywhere?"

"It is cool."

They laughed together.

"Thanks." Tommy flipped on the hallway and porch light.

"Anytime. That's what friends are for." Mona started to turn around, then stopped. "I'm going to leave a few bags on the porch. For your mom's boyfriend. Just a little Halloween treat. Don't touch them, okay? It's for him only."

Tommy looked wary again. "What's in it?"

"A fun Halloween treat. Make sure to stop by our house tomorrow. We have loads of candy."

Then she pulled the three bags from her pocket and set them in front of the door, having faith the guy would show up and see them since Tommy turned on the lights. She winked at Tommy and walked away.

He had no idea, but he just made a very good friend.

Everybody should be friends with a witch.

NICE TEAMWORK

Bozo growled and Scatter hissed. All Mason could do was stand there with his back to what he assumed was a chupacabra. He had heard another growl, one he'd never heard before.

"Peter..."

"Be still."

Peter's hand clutched the bottle Mona had given him, yet he made no move to throw.

"What are you doing?" Mason whispered harshly. He felt like they needed to attack. Not just stand here waiting for it to attack them first.

"I ain't good in situations like this."

Oh, great. Out of all the vampires, he got stuck with the wimp. How in the hell did that happen?

He wanted to turn around. Peter shook his head, barely, but enough to tell Mason not to move. Well, shit. He couldn't just stand here with his back to the beast. He needed to assess the situation, especially if Peter wasn't going to do anything.

"How big is it?"

"Big enough. About four feet or so. It does not look happy. It also looks hungry."

Meow.

Mason looked down at Scatter.

According to Scatter, it had a small meal. Probably a rabbit. He didn't recall seeing a rabbit, but it would explain the blood he found near Tommy's house.

"Okay, you'll be proud of me. I apologized to Tommy, and we're friends now. Did you know that..." Mona's voice trailed off as she stopped frozen in her tracks. Her eyes grew round as she stared behind him.

"Mason, there's a chupacabra behind you."

"Yes, my sweet Mona, so I'm told."

"Don't be moving anymore, Mona," Peter whispered.

"How long do you want me to stand like this, Peter?" Mason demanded.

Peter shrugged.

"We got this."

Mason glanced at Mona, the fierce determination on her face with a piece of licorice dangling from her lips. She held the samurai sword high, her grip firm.

Damn right, they got this. They were together. They always defeated evil together.

"Peter, when I say so, throw the bottle." He looked at Peter, waiting for confirmation he understood, then he glanced at Mona. "We got this."

Raising the ax, tightening his grip, he said a small prayer this would end well.

"Now!"

Peter lobbed the potion bottle into the air. Mason saw it hit its target as he swung around. The chupacabra roared, clawing in the air as it prepared to move forward and attack.

Its fangs looked sharp and deadly as it snarled. He heard Mona running toward the beast just as he did.

They both jerked to a stop when the beast stumbled, made a weird gurgling sound, then its head fell cleanly from its body. The rest of its body followed suit, tumbling to the ground.

Joe and Donnie stood behind it, both wearing shit-eating grins. Joe held a sword coated in blood.

"Nice teamwork," Donnie said, pride in his voice. "Peter, clean it up."

Then he stepped around the messy body and stopped in front of them.

"Whew, what a night. Who wants a drink?"

Hell, he wanted a double of something. Not blood, of course. Never that. But a double shot of whiskey they had in the cupboard sounded perfect.

"I'll pour," Mona said with eagerness and started walking with Donnie by her side.

He glanced at Peter, who shrugged again.

"I told you I'm no good at situations like this. I be the cleanup guy. I need a shovel."

Then Peter walked away.

Bozo and Scatter still stood by him. He met Joe's gaze.

"How did you sneak up behind that thing?"

"Oh, you all kept its attention quite well. Like Donnie said, nice teamwork. We saw it from the other side of the house and decided to flank it from behind. What did Peter throw at it?"

"A potion Mona made to weaken it."

It all happened so fast, but Mason believed the potion helped, giving Joe and Donnie the perfect opportunity to chop its head off.

"I hope this never happens again."

Joe looked somber.

"What?"

Joe gestured at the dead creature. "This won't be the last to come. Mona's strong and powerful. Other creatures can sense it. We need to beef up security."

Not what Mason wanted to hear.

"And we should start hunting them first."

Also, not what Mason wanted to hear.

"Well, as long as I'm not paired with Peter again, fine."

Joe laughed. "Yeah, he's usually behind us. Should've mentioned that. George is even worse. Why do you think he stayed back at the house?"

"You're vampires."

Joe frowned. "Doesn't mean we can't be scared about things."

"We'll handle this."

Mason turned at George's soft tone. The man always spoke softly. He held a shovel. Peter stood next to him holding one as well.

He wasn't going to argue.

With Bozo and Scatter by his side, he headed toward the front of the house. He glanced at Tommy's house when he heard a loud moan.

A large man shoved Tommy aside and rushed inside the house.

Not on his watch. Not to a kid.

Mason took off running, grabbing Tommy by the shoulders when he reached the porch.

"You okay? Was that your mom's boyfriend? Did he hurt you? I saw him shove you."

A slow grin appeared on Tommy's face. "He had to go to the bathroom. I was standing in his way."

"What?"

Tommy shrugged, laughing. "He farted loud and then clutched his stomach and moaned, then ran inside like he was going to die." He frowned. "He's not going to die, is he?"

"I don't think so. Why do you ask?"

Tommy pointed at the porch. Mason looked, eyeing three small bags that looked very familiar. Too familiar.

"Mona said they were for him and not to touch them."

Mason recalled Mona talking about making friends with Tommy. Apparently, she decided to show how friendly she could be. This, he would not complain about. The guy sounded like a dick. The first chance Mason got, he'd talk with Tommy's mom, see just how much of an asshole the guy was. Because if he found out he beat on Tommy—or her —Mason wouldn't hesitate to have Mona whip up some more potions and spells.

"She's a witch, isn't she?"

Mason clamped a hand on Tommy's shoulders and smiled. "She's your friend. Just as I am. As soon as he's done using the bathroom—which might be a while—let me know and I'll escort him out."

Tommy nodded, eyeing the bags once more, before heading back inside.

Mason looked at the bags as well. There was no way he was touching them. Mona could come back to pick them up.

What a night.

He was ready for that drink.

HAPPY HALLOWEEN

MONA READJUSTED HER HAT, trying to find the best position. One where it didn't ruin her hair too much, but enough where it wouldn't fall off. Then she grabbed the black makeup paint and added a large mole near her mouth, on top of the green she had spread across her face.

Yeah, she was a real witch, but she wanted to have fun tonight. It was Halloween. What better costume than dressing up as a witch. A green, wicked witch with a large mole near her mouth. Positively evil, ugly looking witch. She couldn't wait to scare the kids.

In a good way, of course. In the Halloween spirit. Not in a truly evil way. They were friends now.

She—along with Mason's help—got rid of Tommy's boyfriend. The disgusting human being that he was. Beating women and children like he'd keep getting away with it. Of course, they didn't get rid of him in the buried-him-in-the-backyard sense. Nope. They went the legal way. Mason spoke with Tommy's mom, who decided to finally make a police report that he liked to hurt her. Tommy confessed he hit him as well. She had no idea. Mona felt bad for her. A single mom trying to do her best, working two jobs. She, unfortunately, fell into a trap and got scared, unsure of how to get out of it.

Well, problem solved.

Mason arrested him—after the asshole could actually walk away from the toilet without squirting the shits out. Mona reassured her she'd keep an eye on Tommy while she worked nights, and surprisingly, Tommy didn't argue.

So, yeah, they were friends.

Mona walked out of the bathroom and laughed when she saw Joe and Donnie standing by the coffin in their Dracula costumes, drops of blood running down their chins.

"Where's Peter and George?"

Donnie scrunched his nose, shaking his head. "They don't like crowds. We'll help hand out candy, though. It's been a while since I could show my fangs off and not worry about getting a stake to the heart."

"Well, they should start showing up soon. The sun is going down."

"We'll hang back until it goes down," Joe said with a grin.

He winked, and they walked out of the room. She shrieked when a pair of arms circled her, then relaxed when she realized it was Mason. Geez, who else would it be?

Turning around, she giggled when she saw his face. It was painted all white, as was his hair. He wore a white long-sleeve shirt with a pair of white pants.

"What are you supposed to be?"

He stepped back and turned in a complete circle. "A ghost. You're playing a witch, so I thought I should play something I used to be."

"It's an odd way to dress for it. Most people would just throw a sheet over themselves and cut holes for their eyes."

"Well, I'm not most people." He pulled her back into his arms, kissing her. "Most people, if they were really a witch, wouldn't dress up like one either."

"Good thing I'm not most people either."

"Have I told you how much I love you today?"

She shook her head as a wide smile spread across her lips. "Feel free to say it as often as you like."

"You know once the holiday is over, we have to talk about what happened. How we're going to prepare when something like this happens again."

She put a finger to his lips. "But the holiday isn't over. It hasn't even begun."

And she wasn't ready for that talk. That monsters and creatures from around the world would be coming for her. Because she was starting to use her powers. Because she was probably stronger than even she realized.

It had to be the reason why her mother hid this life from her. She had been trying to keep her safe. It was too late for that. The only thing they could do was prepare and be armed.

The doorbell rang.

She squealed with delight. Mason laughed, sharing a look with Scatter and Bozo who were set up comfortably on their pet beds. They'd stick around for a while to watch the show and see the cool costumes the kids came up with.

Mona answered the door, cackling with finesse. "Enter if you dare."

Tommy and his two friends hesitated, then Tommy squared his shoulders and entered first. His friends followed.

"Nice costume. You're a witch."

Mona raised a brow as she looked at Tommy. "Tonight I am. You look pretty cool yourself."

He was dressed as a pirate. Mona had even let him borrow her samurai sword, where he promised to keep it in its scabbard. Because Mona didn't quite trust him enough yet—he was a kid, curiosity would get the better of him—she put a spell on it where he wouldn't be able to pull it out. It'd also give him something to wonder why he couldn't remove the sword. She just couldn't help herself. But it was a pretty awesome detail added to his costume. His two friends were dressed up as Superman and a zombie.

Mona then drew their attention to the coffin and lifted the lid. Although it was brand new, Joe made it so it creaked every time it opened. A nice little added effect.

"Pick your poison." Then she cackled again.

This time Tommy didn't hesitate. He opened his bag and cupped his hands to scoop a large portion into his bag. His friends followed suit.

"So, the place isn't haunted?" Tommy asked, laughing.

"Not anymore it isn't." Mona winked.

Tommy stared at her.

Then Mason stepped up. "Have fun tonight. Don't be afraid to come back for another round. Mona went overboard with the candy."

Tommy nodded and smiled. "Pretty cool place. Thanks for everything."

Then the boys left.

Mason walked closer, sweeping a hand behind her back. "You're not going to cackle in front of every kid, are you? And pick your poison. Really?"

"It's Halloween. Let me have fun."

And Mason did just that.

———

DO YOU WANT TO SEE MORE OF MONA & MASON? THEY ALSO APPEAR IN MY **HAUNTING LOVE SERIES**! CHECK OUT THE FIRST BOOK, THIRD TIME'S THE CHARM!

FOR AN EXCITING ROMANTIC SUSPENSE SERIES
THIRD TIME'S THE CHARM
A HAUNTING LOVE NOVEL, #1

He's not running this time...

Kade thought nothing could be worse than when his wife died in a car accident—especially because he'd been behind the wheel. To forget the pain, he moved on. Maybe too quickly. Now he's the prime suspect in the death of his second wife. But they have nothing on him because he didn't kill her.

Buying a house that needs more repairs than it's worth seems like a good escape. When he meets Bailey, despite everything telling him to look away, guard his heart, he can't help but fall under her charm. There's just one problem. She's a ghost. There can't be any harm in loving a ghost, right? Nothing can hurt her, not even him. Except there's another presence in the house. One that terrifies her.

Between contending with a pesky detective determined to peg him for murder, a ghost he's falling in love with, and the mysterious accidents that keep happening to him at work, Kade fears he might be joining Bailey on the other side sooner rather than later.

For Breck & Charly's story, check out
Thirteen Days Gone
A Haunting Love Novel, #2

A ticking clock. A vision of her own demise.

Psychic Charly Yarrow's curse is about to turn deadly. Ever since she was young, her visions of past and future have haunted her—but never has she foreseen her last day on earth. In thirteen days, the killer will come for her.

Charly's only lifeline is stern Detective Breck Holstrom, though at first he doubts her unique abilities...until the evidence proves uncanny. Determined, he vows to unravel the cryptic clues in her vision to stop her fate.

Drawn together in a race against time with a serial killer's twisted game, Breck battles his skepticism while fighting an undeniable attraction. Charly wants to trust him to help her cheat death and solve the mystery shrouding her murder. But she knows better—her visions always come true. As the encroaching deadline creeps closer, Charly must risk trusting Breck with her life...and her heart.

Don't miss this nail-biting paranormal romantic suspense guaranteed to keep you guessing until the final chapter.

The predator is about to become the prey...

Detective Stella Waters hunts supernatural killers, moving town to town protecting people from evils they don't know exist. When her latest case points to a vampire killer, she doesn't need co-workers interfering. They wouldn't survive a bloodsucking creature.

Donnie is haunted by nightmares of his dark past. He's accepted he'll always live in permanent darkness, but he refuses to let the deadly impulses control him anymore. When innocent people start dying, he's determined to stop the killer terrorizing his town.

Stella knows Donnie is a vampire, but not the one she's hunting. Despite their mutual distrust, they reluctantly join forces. She plans to move on once the case is closed, but there's an inexplicable pull between them neither can deny. As they close in on their suspect, they discover something far more sinister lurking in the shadows—a force that could destroy them both.

Get a taste of this pulse-pounding paranormal romantic suspense where love bites back and danger lurks in every shadow.

0:05...0:04...0:03...0:02...
Bang. Boom.

Isabella Thorn has lived her life with vision after vision, trying to help save people when she can. Of course, not all can be saved. Her latest vision hits her so strong, she's out for hours. Worse, she sees Detective Bo Chapman, the only man to ever capture her heart, shoot her to save other people from the bomb strapped to her chest. Now she must come face-to-face with Bo to warn him what's coming. Something so vicious and brutal, she's not sure she'll survive. He'll need to make a choice: let the bomb blow, or kill her to save everyone else.

Note: This romantic suspense/psychic short story was born out of my weekly flash fiction I write. The first few chapters are from my flashes. I hope you enjoy this short thrilling story!

ABOUT THE AUTHOR

I'm a *USA Today* Bestselling Author that loves to write contemporary romance and romantic suspense novels, although I am partial to romantic suspense. I even dabble in paranormal. Honestly, I love anything that has to do with romance. As long as there's a happy ending, I'm a happy camper. And insta-love...yes, please! I love baseball (Go Twins!) and creating awesome crafts. I graduated with a Bachelor's Degree in Criminal Justice, working in that field for several years before I became a stay-at-home mom. I have a few more amazing stories in the works. If you would like to learn more about me and my books, head to my website by scanning the QR code. Thanks for reading!

Scan me